WINGFIELD'S HOPE

WINGFIELD'S HOPE

More Letters from Wingfield Farm

DAN NEEDLES

KEY PORTER BOOKS

Library and Archives Canada Cataloguing in Publication

Needles, Dan
    Wingfield's hope : more letters from Wingfield Farm / Dan Needles.

Sequel to: Letters from Wingfield Farm.
ISBN 978-1-55263-695-4 (bound).—ISBN 978-1-55263-789-0 (pbk.)

    I. Title.

PS8577.E333W55 2005   C813'.54   C2005-902767-3

THE CANADA COUNCIL | LE CONSEIL DES ARTS
FOR THE ARTS | DU CANADA
SINCE 1957 | DEPUIS 1957

ONTARIO ARTS COUNCIL
CONSEIL DES ARTS DE L'ONTARIO

The publisher gratefully acknowledges the support of the Canada Council for the Arts and the Ontario Arts Council for its publishing program. We acknowledge the support of the Government of Ontario through the Ontario Media Development Corporation's Ontario Book Initiative.

We acknowledge the financial support of the Government of Canada through the Book Publishing Industry Development Program (BPIDP) for our publishing activities.

Key Porter Books Limited
Six Adelaide Street East, Tenth Floor
Toronto, Ontario
Canada M5C 1H6

www.keyporter.com

Text design: Ingrid Paulson
Electronic formatting: Jean Lightfoot Peters

Printed and bound in Canada

07 08 09 10 11   5 4 3 2 1

To Heath
(again and again)

PREFACE

Walt Wingfield owes his creation as a fictional character to a moment of high drama and enormous personal risk in my early career, or to be precise, before I actually had a career. I was knocking about the farm one summer after university, trying to decide what to do with my life, and—just for the hell of it—I harnessed a pair of saddle horses to an old plow. Then I hooked them up to an ancient farm wagon with rickety wooden wheels and a broken seat.

On the first trip down the lane, one of the wheels collapsed and the wagon lurched drunkenly to the right. The horses spooked and took off, the lines snapped, and all I could do was hang onto the rapidly disintegrating wagon like John Carradine in that famous runaway scene in *Stagecoach*. We made one heart-pounding lap of the hayfield and returned to the barn, the horses lathered in sweat and the wagon reduced to kindling. But I survived to tell the story.

That incident had an enormous effect on me. It persuaded me that, instead of trying to farm with horses, I might be safer to go to the typewriter and tell the story of someone else trying to farm with horses. I wrote out a few columns on the subject and sold the concept of the "Letter from Wingfield Farm" to the owner of the local weekly newspaper. And so I became a writer.

I have been exploring Persephone Township for three decades now. The early newspaper columns eventually found their way to the stage and developed a life of their own. With the help of editors like Rod and Doug Beattie, Rick Archbold, Tom Cruickshank, Peter Gredig, Steven Thomas, Jan Walter, Meg Taylor and my wife, Heath, I have ventured far beyond the Seventh Line, into Larkspur and Port Petunia to explore the obscure corners of this peculiar part of the world. These literary "crop tours" have taken us up the Petunia Valley Sideroad, over the Great Rift to the Pluto Sales Barns and back to the Demeter Downs Racetrack, with the occasional pause for reflection and spiritual refreshment in the pews of St. Stephen's-on-the-Drumlin Anglican Church or the bar of the Commercial Hotel in Larkspur. The result is a collection of plays, books and magazine columns that, like the institutions just mentioned, all seem to have generated their own followings and who rely on word of mouth and the Coming Events section of the Larkspur *Free Press & Economist* to connect with each other.

I'm sorry about the confusion; I certainly didn't plan it this way. It just happened. I'm happy to give directions if I bump into you at the store, but failing that, if you would like to know more about the neighbourhood you can always pick up the first volume of Walt's *Letters from Wingfield Farm* or browse the official local history of Persephone Township, *With Axe & Flask*.

WINGFIELD UNBOUND

A note from the editor:
When people call me up here at the newspaper office, I always ask them how things are going. A lot of them say, "Well, I can't complain." But they always find a way. I'm not saying all the calls and letters we get here are complaints. Some of them are lawsuits.

Just listen to this humdinger:

Dear Sir,

As we stand at the threshold of a new century, what hope can there be for the fate of mankind? Anarchists strike at the very heart of civilization, our youth lack any sense of direction, and each day the newspapers carry fresh stories of appalling murder and violence in the streets.

That is dated Larkspur, September 21, 1905.

I'll have to use it in my weekly column, "One Hundred Years Ago Today." I firmly believe that those who forget history are condemned to repeat the mistakes of the past. Knowing our history gives us the opportunity to make entirely new mistakes.

I always assumed I was the only one who read this column, until I dropped it a couple of months ago. There was a great outcry...from one person, Walt Wingfield. And I can't afford to antagonize Walt, because he fills the other side of the page, with the "Letter from Wingfield Farm." Everybody reads that.

Walt Wingfield is an ex-chairman of the board turned farmer. He used to be Chairman and Chief Executive Officer of McFeeters Bartlett & Hendrie—a big brokerage house down on Bay Street. Three years ago he bought a hundred acres out on the Seventh Line of Persephone Township and tried to make a living as a farmer. Since then he has taken a lot of the pressure off me to find news stories about economic catastrophe and property damage.

Last year he married Maggie, the girl next door. She left a life of hard work and poverty on the farm she shared with her brother, Freddy, and settled down to a life of hard work and poverty with Walt. Walt eventually reached a career compromise. He now works part-time at the brokerage to subsidize his part-time farming.

I asked him how he'd compare the two professions. Walt said, "In farming the insider information is legal, but it's much harder to come by."

For the first three seasons, Walt was obsessed with the prospect that he would eventually have to admit defeat and slink back to the city with his tail between his legs. He still has his fits and furies, usually after some spectacular meltdown in the barn or a public humiliation on the sideroad with his unpredictable horses. But I'm happy to say that his old anxiety about making a success of the farm is fading into memory. Now it's been replaced by a new and more powerful anxiety.

The first letter he sent to me after his honeymoon went like this...

March 15

Dear Ed,

I left the office early today and caught the train out of the city, back to Larkspur. Maggie had a dinner meeting of the Women's Institute to get ready for and she was expecting me home to do chores.

It used to bother me that the whole train has to be stopped in Larkspur just to let me off. Then it carries on up to Port Petunia before going back to the city. Tonight, as soon as I stepped off, the locomotive shifted gears and chugged back the way it came. It appears that if I stop riding the train, we won't have one.

The station is boarded up now and the parking lot is usually deserted, except for whoever comes to pick me up. This evening there was no sign of Maggie, which puzzled me because she is always punctual. The only vehicle in the lot was a ten-wheel Freightliner tractor trailer. A sign mounted above the grille said "Kick butt!" There was a blast from the air horns and Maggie leaned out the window.

"Come on, Walt! I'm late!" she shouted.

I jumped up on the running board, grabbed the passenger door handle and hauled myself into the cab. Maggie popped the clutch and we went lumbering out onto Wellington Street.

"The Institute supper starts at six. I've got to get the casserole over to the hall."

"It's a big casserole, is it?"

Maggie smiled at me. "The 4×4 heated up this morning on the way back from the station. I took it in to Ron's and he said the water pump was gone on it."

"So, where did this come from?" I asked.

"This is Ron's loaner. I like it. It's big, but it sure gets around in the snow."

"Will we be driving this to the dinner tonight?"

"No, the 4×4 should be fixed by now. And it's a supper, Walt, not a dinner. Dinner is in the middle of the day."

I'm learning a whole new vocabulary since I married Maggie. A thin cow is said to be "gant" and a day with no wind is "cam." You don't "do" dishes, you "redd them up."

"Right, I forgot," I said. "But you're not dressed." Maggie was wearing blue jeans and a white cotton blouse.

It turned out that the pipes had frozen upstairs in the empty apartment above the store she rents for her dress shop, but they didn't notice until the heat of the day thawed them out again and water started coming through the ceiling. I guess it made a real mess, because her assistant Bernice was still mopping up. Maggie pointed at two parcels on the floor of the truck.

"I have to deliver these two orders, get back and close up, but it's going to take me another hour. So, I want you to take the 4×4 down to the farm, do the chores, iron my blue dress, leave it on the door and take the casserole up to the hall. I'll meet you there. Oh, and feed Spike."

Spike the hound started life next door with Maggie and her brother, Freddy, as an outside dog. In my first year here he defected to my place and became an inside dog. When I carried Maggie over the threshold she carried Spike back outside. This remains a bone of some contention between them. Maggie wheeled into Ron's garage and rolled down the window.

She leaned out the window and yelled, "Is that water pump done, Ronnie?"

Ron was standing in the doorway, wiping his hands on an oily rag. "Done like a dinner, Maggie," he said. "But we got you goin'. Found you a low mileage replacement from the road superintendent's truck. He won't be needin' his until after the Good Roads Convention."

Maggie turned back to me. "Now, Walt, do you remember what you have to do?"

This was always a tricky moment. I recited the list carefully to her: take the 4×4 down to the farm, do the chores, iron the dress...

"The blue dress," she interrupted.

"...yes, the blue dress...leave it on the door and take the casserole up to the hall. You'll meet me there...oh, and feed Spike."

Maggie smiled again. "Good...nice to see you, dear." She leaned over and gave me a smooch. I climbed out of the Freightliner and Maggie roared off.

Ron grinned at me from the doorway. "The keys are in it, Walt. I haven't got a bill done for you. We'll catch up to you later."

Maggie calls it "the casserole," but it isn't like any casserole you or I were brought up on. It's more of a ham and egg pie, and it is delicious. We hardly ever get it at home because Maggie gets asked to make it for every big dinner out...I mean, supper. As the 4×4 bumped down the lane at the farm, I could almost smell it cooking.

But as soon as I opened the door, I could see something was wrong. There in the middle of the kitchen carpet was Maggie's good casserole dish...licked clean, and Spike was standing beside it.

"Spike! Did you eat Maggie's casserole?" Spike's ears drooped even lower and he hung his head. "I'll take that as a yes," I said sternly. "And I hope confession is good for your soul. You know what Maggie will say. You'll be an outside dog...with no chance of parole...for life. And I may be out there with you." Spike ears drooped and he flopped to the floor.

This was serious. What was I going to do about the dinner? I phoned Freddy, Maggie's brother, who lives on the farm next door. He's been getting by with a part-time housekeeper since Maggie and I were married last year. We're on the party line, which means I have to hold the receiver down and listen to my phone ring about nineteen times. When it stops it means Freddy has finally picked up the line. On this occasion it stopped after nine rings.

"Hyello! How are you now, Walt?"

"Fine...well, not so fine. Spike just ate the casserole Maggie made for the Institute."

"Gollies!" he chuckled. "He's not even a member, is he?"

"This isn't funny, Freddy. You know how Maggie is about the Institute. Would she have any of her old recipe books up at your place? The dinner starts in an hour and a half!"

"It's a supper, Walt. Dinner's in the middle of the day. But come on up. I lived with that woman for thirty-seven years. I know all her recipes. We'll put it together for you."

In nine minutes flat I was standing in Freddy's kitchen. In the old days, when Maggie lived here, the kitchen was the only place on Freddy's farm where anything actually worked. But in the short six months since Maggie left, the jungle has reclaimed its own. It looks like the set for *Cats*. Dishes piled in the sink, newspapers stacked on every chair. The dinner table has become a workbench and boxes of beer bottles are stacked against the wall. I suggested as delicately as I could that maybe we should try putting the casserole together down at my place.

"Naw, naw," he said, waving away my objections. "Just clear away a spot here. I remember how this thing goes. First you gotta have toast, lots of toast. You brought the eggs and the ham?"

"Right here. Do you cook the noodles first?"

"No, you just put in lots of water. How long is this thing supposed to cook?"

"It says an hour at 350 degrees."

"We're a little tight for time, Walt. Let's try half an hour at 700."

"Stoves don't go that high, Freddy."

"Actually, this one does if you put it on self-clean."

In ten minutes we had it slammed together and in the oven, which has to be a record, even for Maggie. When it was cooked, I rushed it out to the 4×4—waved a thank you to Freddy and blasted through the snow to the hall. At thirteen minutes past six I jogged up the steps of the Orange Hall and met Maggie, coming out of the cloakroom with a casserole dish in her hands. Her eyes widened in The Look, which is a strong indicator that what is on her mind can't be said out loud in public.

"There you are! What a relief!" she said in a tone that indicated she was feeling no relief at all. "I thought you'd gone into the ditch somewhere. Where on earth have you been? And what is that?"

"You wanted me to pick up the casserole..."

"I got the casserole myself, Walt. But when I got there, my dress wasn't ironed, the chores weren't done, and Spike was looking at me as if he hadn't been fed. Hello, Vi." She handed off her casserole to Violet McKeown and turned back, and her voice dropped again.

"Did you remember anything I said?"

"I thought Spike ate the casserole. He was licking out the dish when I came into the kitchen...Hi, Victor!" I waved at the superintendent of the Sunday school.

"That was some toast I put down for him after breakfast," she whispered. "The casserole was in the oven. I have more than one casserole dish, Walt. Now, what is that? Hi, Bernice." She smiled at the lady who delivers our mail.

"Freddy and I made another casserole. So, now we have two...Frank. How are you?" I nodded to the man who lives in the white house beside the church in Larkspur.

Maggie raised the lid on the casserole dish and examined the contents. "It looks...it looks lovely, Walt." Her voice dropped again to a whisper. "Take that back out to the 4×4...right now."

It was a beautiful supper. Maggie looked divine in her blue dress. Her casserole vanished in seconds. She was reinstalled as Treasurer. Outgoing President Elsie Burton was honoured for delivering her ten thousandth meal on wheels for seniors. She was too shy to say anything but "thank yez all very much," and she was thrilled with her prize, which was a three-day bus trip to Nashville.

Spike got his kibble a little later than usual that night. We tried him on Freddy's casserole, but he couldn't eat it. Still, Freddy and I have decided to hang on to the recipe. We think we may have invented a new roofing material.

Yours sincerely,
Walt

April 15
Dear Ed,

I've acquired horses in descending order of mobility. My first, Feedbin, is actually quite spirited, though erratic. My second, Mortgage, is not a self-starter and would rather stay in the barn. Once on the move, though, she can do as much damage as Feedbin. My third is an old draft horse named King who hardly ever moves at all. If I buy another horse, it will have to be a statue.

I have no idea how old these horses are. Going down to the stable now is like going to the Legion. Feedbin's all grey around the muzzle, Mortgage has the beginnings of white-eye, and King...well...I understand if King lives another year he'll get a letter from the Queen.

This morning I decided to get Mortgage and Feedbin out with the buggy. I may be pushing the season a bit, but it's been a long winter and I figured it would do us all good to get the adrenalin flowing.

25 Sideroad is a tricky drive at this time of the year. Where the road follows the river you have to watch for people like Don, my dairy-farming neighbour to the south, who drives along the wrong side of the road, leaning out his window, scanning the creek for fish. This morning I could see him meandering along towards us after we

turned the corner from the Seventh Line. Thankfully, he saw us in time. He yanked his truck back over to his side of the road and passed us. Then he pulled a U-turn in the intersection and came up alongside.

"So, how are you findin' married life, Walt?" he asked in that solemn, slow drawl he has.

"No complaints, Don. I'm a lucky man."

"We'll get you out here in a couple of weeks with a fly rod, Walt. Then we'll see if you're a lucky man. How're the horses?"

"So far so good. But if this is a visit, I think I'll tie them up to the road sign here."

I gingerly descended from the buggy, keeping a tight rein on the horses, and led them over to a new post the road department had installed at the intersection. It sported a bright new green sign with an unfamiliar name on it.

"What's this, Don?" I asked. "Regional Road Number Four? Is this some kind of joke?"

Don seemed puzzled by it, too. "Well, how about that?" he said. "I guess it's part of the restructuring."

"Restructuring?"

"Yeah, they got numbers now for all the roads."

"They *had* numbers. That's the Seventh Line. This is 25 Sideroad."

Don shrugged. "Thing of the past, Walt. They're putting all the townships together...Larkspur, too. They're gonna make one big local government, called the Region of Hillview."

"Hillview? When did all this happen?"

"It's been in the paper every week for about six months, Walt."

"That's unbelievable, Don. The township has been here for 125 years. It's the oldest continuous form of government in the country. How can they just do away with it?"

"C'mon, Walt. No one is goin' to miss it. It wasn't much more than a dry place to play cards. That's why I got off the council."

Don ran for council after the big controversy over the Persephone Glen condominium development across the road from my farm. We managed to stop that particular monstrosity, but Don soon found that the township doesn't have any control over development anymore. Anyone with deep pockets and good lawyers can build anything he wants, anywhere. In the past few years, monster homes have sprouted like mushrooms on the top of every drumlin between here and Highway 13. "View properties" they call them.

"But the history," I protested. "And the motto on the township crest: *'Passim arborem horarem luserunt.'* The changing trees are the guides to the seasons."

"Is that what it means?" said Don. "I always thought it meant 'Pass the bower, lose for an hour.'"

"Don, don't you see what's happening? Without history we have no memory. We're losing all the old signposts."

"You've taken down a few signposts yourself with them horses, Walt," said Don.

I glanced around and saw that we were blocking the road for an ancient Dodge pickup that belongs to my neighbour across the road—the Squire. Up here, when vehicles block the road it doesn't mean there is an obstruction. It means the meeting is called to order. The Squire must be close to eighty now, and he's all crippled up with arthritis. It was painful to watch him ease himself out of the cab and hobble around to lean on the fender.

"G'day, fellas. What's the matter with these horses, Walt? I never seen them stand in one place so long without busting somethin'. Say, is that horse goin' white in the eye?"

"The vet says she may be going blind," I replied. "He doesn't think there's much you can do about it at her age."

The Squire pushed away from the truck and looked Mortgage in the eye.

"You've great faith in the veterinarian, Walter. When I kept livestock I had more faith in the tobacconist. You can treat a horse with drugs all you want, but tobacco is the stuff that cures him. We used to give a horse chewing tobacco for the worms."

"And they swallowed it? That stuff's poison."

"I know," said the Squire. "Killed the worms dead. Never seemed to hurt the horses much. Of course, it is habit forming, but in them days it didn't cost that much to support a horse's tobacco habit. Whenever old Peanut flared up with the white-eye, I just spit tobacco juice in his eye, three times a day for a week; cleared it up every time. And the surprising thing is, we stayed friends... Anyway, you should ask Jimmy to come down and have a look at her."

Don and I looked at each other. Old Jimmy, Freddy's hired man, was the expert on horses around here for many years, but he died two years ago. Maybe the Squire meant someone else.

"Jimmy?" I ventured.

"Yeah, Jimmy knows the horses." The Squire nodded his head once quickly to punctuate the observation in that way he has, to signal that no further discussion is required.

"But Jimmy's dead," I said.

"Jimmy died two years ago," said Don.

The Squire tilted his head and frowned at the sun as if he just realized he'd left his wallet on the kitchen table. "I know that," he said impatiently. "I know that. I just meant you shoulda asked him if he was here, that's all. If you guys'll clear a path I gotta move on."

He shuffled off back to his truck, climbed in and drove off without a wave.

"Now what was that all about?" I wondered.

Don shrugged. "He's been getting confused lately, Walt. Kinda livin' in the past, I guess. Not surprising, considering the age he is now."

"I've noticed he talks more and more about the past. And the stories he can tell..."

Don raised his right eyebrow, which is the one he uses to indicate skepticism. "Well, that stuff about the horses is true," he said. "But some of the stuff he talks about now...I don't know where it comes from. Well, I gotta go. Do you want me to hold on to these guys while you get squared away?"

"Good idea."

Don held the bridles while I climbed back in the buggy. He stepped back, I gave a little cluck, and we clattered off again. But it wasn't the same. The conversation had put a damper on the day. I know the Squire can't live forever, but he's like a barometer for so much I see around me.

You know, for the first few years up here the biggest question on my mind was whether I could make a go of the farm and keep my head above water. Now that Maggie and I have worked out a balance between my work and hers, the future of the farm looks pretty straightforward. It's all the other ones around me that I worry about. Everywhere I look I see signs that the old rural community of Persephone Township is disintegrating. Half the farms have been sold because the owners have died or retired or just given up. The new owners are city people like myself, but they have no interest in farming. The barns stand empty, the fences have collapsed. And now this restructuring business. Fair Persephone displaced by the thudding dullness of "Hillview." Imagine what the committee looked like that came up with that clanger!

It's not just the Squire who's losing his memory, it's the whole community. It's not fair. It seems that just at the moment when I finally arrive at the place in life where I've always wanted to be, it decides to fall apart around me.

It should have been a great day for an outing. Water gushed in the ditches, the sun lifted the moisture off the horses' backs, and the air carried that distinctive spring smell...all those little furry things the coyotes had been eating all winter were thawing out. I decided to head upwind.

The drive down the Centre Road towards Hollyhock is one that never fails to lift my spirits. As you crest the first hill, you get a panoramic view of the Boyne River Valley through a picture frame of white cedars. The drumlins spill down like eggs out of a basket, with the tiny village of Hollyhock nestled at the bottom. It never was a busy place, but now it's like a cemetery with street lights. Doctors and dentists from the city who appear only on weekends have renovated the old houses. During the week, nothing stirs. You could say that Hollyhock has fallen on good times.

There's a bend in the river here and a pretty waterfall that tumbles into a dramatic gorge. An abandoned stone grist mill stands above it, and the old millstone lies on its side in midstream at the bottom. If these stones could talk, what stories they could tell...

Then it came to me. This would be the perfect place to preserve a glimpse of the old rural community. It could be restored as a museum where people could bring their children and grandchildren. Then, at least, if the old ways have to die, they won't have vanished without a trace. The foundations still looked sound and there was plenty of stone lying about to use in a new structure. A voice from behind me interrupted my thoughts.

"Hi there. It's Walt Wingfield, isn't it?"

I turned to see Dr. Winegard, a dentist who used to be one of my clients in the city. He was bouncing a basketball with his teenage son on the asphalt driveway of his renovated stone farmhouse. He threw the ball to his son and trotted over.

"Traded stocks for livestock, have you, Walt? Heh, heh. This is great. I just love horses. Chip, come and see the horses."

He walked straight up to Mortgage, who was tossing her head irritably, and reached out a hand.

"Ah, I wouldn't do that—" I cautioned him.

Mortgage pulled her lips back and grabbed the cuff of his sports jacket with her teeth.

Dr. Winegard jumped back and checked to see that the brass buttons were still there.

"Whoa, nice horsie..." he laughed nervously. He backed around to the side of the buggy, keeping his eye on Mortgage.

"Good to see you, Dr. Winegard. How's the practice?"

"Oh, you know me, Walt. Drilling, filling and billing. Managed to save enough for a little hobby farm here. I call it 'Tooth Acres.' You get it? Listen, we should get together sometime. Where do you go for lunch up here?"

"To my kitchen usually. I guess there's the Red Hen Restaurant in Larkspur. But they don't do cappuccino. How are your investments?"

"I'm not doing much in the market right now," he said. "I've got all my spare cash tied up in cattle."

I looked around. There were no fences on his little acreage, and the barn had long since disappeared. "Cattle?" I asked. "Where do you keep cattle?"

"Oh, no, not here. Bill Haddock is keeping them for me."

Bill Haddock. I couldn't think of any Bill Haddocks in the neighbourhood. Maggie is a Haddock, and so of course, is Freddy. Must be one the relatives, I thought. Then it struck me.

"Do you mean Willy?" I asked.

"Yes. Very enterprising young man. He and his brother got me a load of western steers. Eighteen-month turnover. I do the money...they do the management."

Willy and Dave are Freddy and Maggie's nephews. In fact, the scary part about marrying Maggie was they suddenly became *my* nephews. They're wonderful fellows if you need tax-free cigarettes or venison...they call it government beef. But I've never thought of them as management material.

However, I kept my thoughts to myself and said goodbye to the dentist. The horses pricked up their ears as we made a wide circle on the road to face north again. I could feel the magnetic pull of the oat bin drawing them back up the hill to the farm.

I'm going to look into this museum business, Ed. It may not be the answer to all our problems, but if I can do some small thing to preserve at least the memory of the old rural community, I feel I owe it to the next generation.

Yours sincerely,
Walt

April 25

Dear Ed,

I went into the sheep pen the other day and noticed one of the ewes lying down in the normal fashion but with her head pulled back and her nose in the air, staring straight up at the ceiling. I tried to get her up, but she couldn't walk. Something was definitely not right, so I called Freddy in for a "consultation." Freddy studied the ewe for a few minutes.

"Mike Fisher had one just like this last summer and he had to shoot it," he said.

"That's terrible. What did she have?"

"I don't know...but it was fatal. I suppose you could give her a shot of B_{12} and drench her with glycol. That sometimes helps a sheep with the staggers."

This did not sound promising. I went to the kitchen to get a second opinion from Maggie. Maggie has a whole cupboard dedicated to veterinary medicine. It is crammed full of pills, potions and lotions, drenching tubes, bandages and disinfectants. There is also an extensive library on the ailments of domestic livestock. The kitchen table has doubled as an operating theatre for small animals on more than one occasion. Maggie reached for her sheep book and flipped through the pages.

"It's not the staggers," she said after a moment. "It sounds more like pregnancy toxemia to me. Give her four cc's of B_{12} and drench her with a half cup of glycol. She should come around by morning. If she doesn't, we'll call the vet."

The ewe did not come around next morning. She was till staring at the ceiling and drooling heavily. The vet doesn't make house calls anymore. So I had to figure some way to get the sheep into town. Freddy offered his truck but shook his head when he arrived.

"Jeez, Walt, I'm not much good at a dead lift anymore. She's gotta weigh over two hundred pounds, and we can multiply that by three if she doesn't want to go."

I had already figured that one out. Using the ancient Egyptian principles of the lever and the inclined plane, Freddy and I dragged the ewe slowly and painfully up a plywood ramp I had constructed and then rolled her as gently as possible onto the bed of the pickup truck.

Freddy wiped his hands on his overalls. "She sure is slobberin' a lot. You don't mind bein' sneezed on by a sheep, do you?"

"Why, is that a good shirt you're wearing?" I laughed.

"Ah, nothin' that won't wash out. Gotta hand it to you, though. You're not squeamish."

By the time the ewe was loaded we were both up to our elbows in sheep slobber. We drove into town and, as we waited at the stoplights, an old man on the bench in front of the drugstore noticed the sheep and glanced up at the sky to see what she was staring at. When the light turned green we left a small crowd of people staring at the sky. At the clinic, the vet came out, took one look at the ewe and put on a pair of rubber gloves.

"What, you don't think she's got rabies, do you?" asked Freddy nervously.

"She is showing some of the symptoms," said the vet. "The virus is carried through the saliva. It's important not to have contact with the saliva. Have you been handling her?"

Freddy looked at me and shrugged. "Don't worry, Walt, I've had the shots lots of times. They just give you one...a day...in the stomach. You get used to it."

"Actually, you take a pill nowadays," said the vet. He took a blood sample from the ewe and told us to call him in the morning for the results. "In the meantime, I can give you some glycol and B_{12}. That might help her."

"We already did that. Thanks, Doc," said Freddy. "We seem to be able to get that stuff cheaper than you do."

Next morning, Freddy came straight over after breakfast. If he was trying to make me feel more optimistic, he failed.

"Was that your sheep I saw chasing the school bus this morning, Walt? You haven't had any problems with uncontrollable thirst, have you?"

"Oh, stop it, Freddy," scolded Maggie. "He didn't sleep a wink last night."

"Actually, her neck is straightened out and she's eating hay. If it was rabies, she wouldn't be doing that, would she?"

"Nope," agreed Freddy. "Rabies isn't the sort of thing you shake off after a coupla days."

We called the vet to report the news. He sounded quite pleased.

"Sounds like you've turned the corner with her, Mr. Wingfield. I think what you're dealing with is a form of sheep polio. Don't worry. It's not contagious and the others aren't likely to get it unless there's a thiamine deficiency in the flock."

"So, what's the treatment from here?"

"The B_{12} mixture you've been giving her has thiamine in it. So just keep it up and pour half a cup of glycol down her throat every six hours."

I thanked him and rang off.

"Well, ain't that a corker?" said Freddy. "We've been through the textbook on sheep ailments from toxemia to polio and the treatment remains the same. Anyway, congratulations, Doctor."

"Let's not count our chickens," I said. "The doctor says she will probably have some brain damage."

"Oh, yeah?" said Freddy. "And, like, how would you tell with a sheep? Their brains run on two penlight batteries. You know, the Double-A size."

"Well, she'll probably get by with Triple-A now."

Over the next few days, it became clear that the ewe was indeed a couple of brain cells short of a full cortex. She didn't recognize me when I came into the stable in the morning. When she came back in from the pasture she looked at the barn in astonishment, as if to say, "When did they build this?" Now, whenever I put hay in the trough, she looks at it closely as if she's never seen hay before.

I understand that a fish never gets bored in an aquarium because each time it swims around the tank it forgets that it's been there before. No matter how many laps it makes, its view of the world remains forever fresh, which would be as close to a blessed state as any creature can achieve in this life. So it is with this sheep.

Yours sincerely,
Walt

April 30

Dear Ed,

Still in the middle of lambing out here, and the results are nothing to boast about.

Maggie is the expert on sheep and she says we really have to buy a ram. She made this pronouncement when Freddy came down for supper last Monday. I have had the sheep for two years now, but I have managed to do so without investing in a ram of my own. Freddy just opens a gate in November and lets his old Corriedale ram into my pasture for a few weeks. Five months later, sometime in April, little lambies appear. I throw terms like "Corriedale," around loosely, but, of course, Freddy's sheep are by no means purebred. Anyway, Freddy was a little prickly about it. He was tilted back in the pressback armchair at our dining-room table when Maggie brought the subject up.

"So, what's the matter with my ram, Maggie?" he asked, gouging one of his molars with a toothpick.

"Well, look at the lambs he throws. They're no good for wool or meat. We could only sell them to vegetarian nudists."

Freddy shrugged. "I'll be the first to say it, they're not fancy sheep, but by gollies, they're tough. Actually, they're more of a hunting sheep. I might use a couple of them up in the county forest this fall to track wolves."

Maggie fluffed out the Hillhurst County Shopper and pointed to the auction notices. "There are some rams listed in tomorrow's sheep auction for the Pluto sales barn," she said.

"Yeah, I saw them," agreed Freddy. "There's always rams up there, Walt. People trade them around this time of the year to kinda freshen up the gene pool."

The Pluto sales barn is a great place to get rid of live-stock, but I've never bought anything there. I'm always leery about bringing some animal health problem back to the farm.

"But sales barns are an incubator for disease," I said. "Don't you ever worry about that?"

"Sure I do," nodded Freddy. "But when I'm over at Pluto I use my elbows to open the washroom doors and I never order anything with gravy on it, if I can help it."

"You can take the 4×4, Walt," said Maggie.

"But will a ram fit in the back of the 4×4?"

Maggie looked at me serenely. "Rams can be dangerous," she said. "If it doesn't fit in the 4×4, don't bring it home."

Gassing up at Ron's in Larkspur the next morning I noticed a tractor-trailer parked across the road. It was car-rying a load of last fall's calves. Not the usual scruffy Shorthorn crossbreeds from the local pasture farms in Persephone Township. These were smooth, fat Limousin calves from the west. A lot of them. I know just enough about cattle to know that I couldn't afford six of these, let alone a hundred. Around the corner of the trailer came Willy and Dave. Willy flashed a gold-toothed smile at me.

"Wanna buy some cattle, Uncle Walt? We can get you in at the special family rate! Aren't they pretty?"

Willy and Dave are two lanky fellows in their mid-twenties with charming manners and high-pitched laughs that sound like the shriek of a startled parrot. They have omnivorous taste in employment. They are self-described "cash-croppers," by which they mean that all of the land they work is rented and they're always short of cash because it's buried in the soil at the moment. But despite all that, they're usually at the wheel of some immense machine, like this huge truck.

"They certainly are pretty," I agreed. "They must be worth a pretty penny."

"Yeah," said Dave. "They'll sure raise the standards around home."

"Oh, of course," I said. "These must be the ones you got for Dr. Winegard, the dentist down in Hollyhock."

Willy glanced at Dave and bobbed his head. "Ah, yeah. Some of these would be his, too, I guess. Say, Walt, we were lookin' at the Chicago price for cattle on your computer. We were wondering how you get into the futures market if you want to make a trade. Do you ever do that?"

I've been introducing Willy and Dave to the fundamentals of the market via my computer. They're keen students and with a bit of coaching they have already done reasonably well with a few simple trades I made for them.

"Well, we can look at that together some day. You have to have the password."

"Password?" said Willy. "Oh, right . . . a password."

Dave elbowed him and climbed up into the cab.

"Come on, Willy," he shouted. "Let's keep these dogies movin'. Rollin' rollin' rollin'... RawHIDE!"

At the Pluto sales barn I scanned the pens and soon found the rams. They were a dreary-looking bunch, with matted wool and patches of bare skin showing. They'd had a hard winter. In the very last pen there was a good candidate: a very tall and noble-looking Oxford ram, all freshly clipped to show off his muscles. He looked like an aging golf pro in long underwear. A ram of this quality would probably bring a high price, but he was worth a try.

I sat in the bleachers, listening to the hum of the sale and waiting for the rams to come out. The first five sold for about fifty dollars each. Then they brought in my Oxford. The auctioneer started the bidding at twenty-five dollars, and I stuck up my hand, bracing for a fight up to two hundred dollars. The auctioneer took my bid, prattled to the crowd for about ten seconds and then pointed to me.

"... twenty-five and a bid now thirty and a bid now thirty and a bid now thirty and... sold for twenty-five dollars. What is your number, sir?"

I was amazed. Twenty-five dollars for a ram like that was a real bargain. This didn't make sense. I rose and trotted down the stairs to have another look at him before they ushered him out of the ring. He walked without a limp, his eyes were clear and he wasn't coughing. Past that you couldn't really tell. He certainly was big. Very big. But he didn't look dangerous. He had a slightly offended look, like a lawyer being asked to wait in line.

As it turned out, I almost needed a shoehorn to get him into the 4×4, but with the help of two attendants we got him loaded. Back at the farm Maggie helped me extract him and put him in the stable.

"Walt," she said. "He's the size of a small horse. Where did he come from?"

I told her the story.

"You got him for twenty-five dollars?" she said, and then put her hand to her mouth. "Oh, my goodness, this must be Floyd McLean's ram."

"Floyd McLean?"

"Floyd McLean farmed in Demeter Township. He had a problem with his nerves. They had him up in Penetang for a while, trying to calm him down. The experts had a theory that the colour pink was good for violent people and they had the whole room and everything in it painted pink. When Floyd came back he was all right, as long as he took his medication, but he always had a problem with the colour pink after that."

"What happened to him?"

"He had another attack in April. Easter was always a difficult time for him. They put him back in the pink room."

"And it didn't work?"

Maggie shook her head sadly. "I guess not. They say he put his head right through the wall. Anyway, he never came out. And the night he died, this ram was born. Folks up in Demeter believe Floyd's soul passed into the ram, and now nobody will touch it. They even named it after him ... Pink Floyd."

The phone rang and Maggie went inside to answer it. I

couldn't believe what I was hearing. It appeared the reason I got this splendid animal for next to nothing is that people imagine he is possessed by the spirit of his owner.

I put my hand under his chin and guided him to the main pen. He came peacefully; I bumped open the pen gate and let go of him. He blinked a couple of times and started chewing his cud. He wasn't hard to manage at all. I went hunting for a couple of sheep gates to block the door, so he could see out without getting out until he was used to his new surroundings.

Of course, what we're dealing with here is an Evil Eye culture—people have all kinds of superstitious beliefs dating back hundreds of years. Some of them make sense. For instance, don't plant until the frogs sing three times—that actually works. But there are others. If you leave new shoes on the table, or dream about a birth, or plow down snow—these all mean certain death. Obviously these are loony notions, like this business with the ram. What perplexes me is that people up here make no attempt to distinguish between taboos against things that are genuinely dangerous and ones against things that are utterly harmless. I finished wiring the sheep gates together, blew my nose on a pink handkerchief and stuffed it in my back pocket. Then I bent over to pick the fence pliers off the floor of the pen.

At the hospital, I was treated for concussion and something with a Latin name that actually just means a pain in the butt. When I woke up, the Squire was sitting in a chair beside the bed.

"How are you now, Walt?" he asked. "I brought you some stuff."

I was expecting him to hand me a newspaper and some of those Western novels he reads. Instead, he opened a cardboard box and pulled a little electric fan out of it. He placed it on the bedside table and plugged it into the wall socket. It made a soft little whirr that was quite soothing.

"This is for when the sun comes around to the west, Walt. It can get stinkin' hot in here. And I got you a fly-swatter, too. It's bad for flies in the evening. And this here's in case you ever need a nurse."

He reached into the box and drew out a large brass school bell.

"There's a call button right here, attached to the bed," I pointed out.

The Squire shook his head. "That's not hooked up to nothing. And I got you some cigarettes…"

"But I don't smoke!"

"Neither do I. They're for when the school bell doesn't work. You light up one of these, you get nurses comin' from all directions."

"Well, thanks," I chuckled. But I was puzzled. "How do you know all this? Have you been in here a lot?"

The Squire shrugged. "I just come in for the usual… you know, plugs, points and condenser. At my age I'm kinda past the warranty."

There was a familiar rustle at the door. Maggie breezed into the room and fluttered a kiss on my forehead. She sat down on the other side of the bed and smiled.

"Hello, dear. I brought you some flowers."

The Squire pulled himself to his feet. "I'll push along now, Walt. And remember, rule number one for the shepherd...never turn your back on a ram." He grinned and shuffled out.

I turned back to Maggie. "So, how is Pink Floyd?"

"He's all right," she smiled. "I decided to start training him. I left your overalls with that pink handkerchief sticking out of the pocket hanging on the concrete gatepost. He's having a sleep now. Are you feeling better, dear?"

"I'm all right. Did you know the Squire is a regular patient here?"

"Just the past couple of years. He gets run down from time to time. None of us lasts forever, Walt."

"I know that...I guess that's why I want to press on with this museum idea. It would help to keep things from disappearing completely. At least we'd have some kind of permanent record of a way of life."

"You may have a permanent record of your encounter with Floyd. When we brought you in here I noticed you had one of your antacid tablets in your overalls pocket where Floyd hit you. It looks like a tattoo—you can actually read it."

"What does it say?"

"It says 'smuT.' It makes it look like I married a biker."

Yours sincerely,
Walt

May 25

Dear Ed,

Maggie's gone for a few days to move her aunt into a chronic care hospital in Barrie. I decided to spend the time seeing what the township council had to say about my museum proposal. I called the township clerk and got a spot on the agenda for the regular meeting on the fourth Thursday of the month. Since Maggie had the 4×4, I borrowed Freddy's truck for the drive.

The township government has been housed in the old Hollyhock schoolhouse for the last forty years. I got there at eight o'clock and let myself in the east door, over which, embossed in the brick, were the words "Boys Entrance." Some wag had painted in front of the inscription the word "Old."

I had been here once before, two years ago, to protest Darcy Dixon's condominium development. They were sitting in exactly the same position as I last saw them. The reeve, wearing his thirty-pound chain of office, sat at the centre of the table, with the deputy reeve on his right and the other councillors on his left. Harold, the clerk, sat at a separate table and prompted the reeve through the agenda. It crossed my mind that we had the makings of a museum right here.

Harold was just starting up the machinery of government as I came in.

"Your worship," he was saying. "We have two applications for permits on the Conservation Area picnic ground. The first is from the Persephone Animal Rights Action Committee."

The reeve scowled and shot a glance towards his deputy. "You got somethin' to say about this, Ernie?" It wasn't a question.

Ernie squared his shoulders and closed his eyes as if someone had just heaved a tomato at him. "I'm agin' it," he said flatly. "Last time I went for my wolf bounty cheque I had to cross their picket line. They spattered me with animal blood. Called me names."

"What's the other one for, Harold?" asked the reeve.

"It's for the Larkspur Rod and Gun Club barbeque, your Worship."

The reeve glanced to his left now, at a man who appeared to be the oldest elected representative in the British Commonwealth. "Wilfrid?" he prompted.

Wilfrid's eyes opened slowly, like a crocodile contemplating a flamingo leg.

"They're just as bad," he hissed. "I had to cross their picket line when I went to register my twelve-gauge. When I came out, my car windshield was soaped."

"Turn 'em both down, Harold," snapped the reeve. Harold paused with his ruler on the page and his pencil poised above it, ready to draw a line through the agenda item.

"Your Worship, might I point out that both applications happen to be for the same date? Might I suggest a motion to grant both permits for the same spot?"

There was another pause while the reeve studied the portrait of Queen Elizabeth and Prince Philip on the wall behind me. He glanced to his left and right and said, "Carried. What have we got next, Harold?"

"Your worship...we have a deputation." He nodded in my direction.

"I can see that, Harold. Mr. Wingfield...nice to have you back before council. I understand you have a proposal for a museum you want us to have a look at."

"Yes, I do."

I stood up and approached the bench. They looked slightly bemused as I plopped a three-page proposal in front of each of them and launched into my presentation. I talked about the rich history of Persephone and the distinctive way of life that makes it such an interesting place to live. Then I moved on to the rapid changes we have seen in the past few years, the loss of farmland to development, how the old family farms are being bought out, the owners retiring and their children looking to other kinds of employment or leaving the township altogether. The demographics of Persephone are changing rapidly and the community's memory of itself is slipping away. I stressed the need for some way to preserve what we know of that old rural community before it is lost forever, and explained how a museum would help.

"And in conclusion, gentlemen, I cannot stress too heavily the benefits of an institution that would preserve the rich history of Persephone Township, a world that I fear is slipping away."

"That sounds like a real fine idea, Mr. Wingfield," said the reeve.

Ernie reached behind him for a large axe leaning up against the wood panelling.

"And I got something here you'd want to have in that museum. Belonged to my dad but I know he'd want to donate it. This here's the axe that was used to clear the first farm in Persephone Township... over here on the Fourth Line in the Back Settlement... woulda been 1836."

"Really?" I said. "That's remarkable. It doesn't look that old."

"Somebody put a new head on it just after the war," said the reeve.

Wilfrid came to life again. "And my father replaced the handle on that axe in 1972," he quavered. "One of the last things he ever did."

"But it's the very same axe," said Ernie, daring the others to contradict him.

Wilfrid placed both hands on the table and raised himself slowly. He was wearing a Sam Browne belt and a scabbard dangled from his side. "Now, if you want some real history," he said, "my great-great-grandfather, who did the first survey of this township, cut his way up through the bush swinging this sword..." With a flourish, he drew a navy cutlass from the scabbard and gave me a shaky salute. The other councillors ducked.

"Careful, Wilfrid," warned the reeve.

Wilfrid leaned over the table, pointing the sword at me. "...the same sword he used to drive the Americans across the Niagara River at Queenston Heights in 1812. The dark spots on that sword are American blood."

"Maybe they are, Wilfrid," said Ernie. "Or maybe Laura Secord's cow peed on it."

"Yeah, well, one thing for sure," said the reeve. "That strongbox Harold uses to keep the minutes in was a gift from the first tax collector sent out by the Lieutenant Governor in 1841."

"Really," I said. "That's an odd gift."

"Gave his horse, too," added Ernie.

"And his watch," cackled Wilfrid. "And a signet ring. And a gold tooth..."

"Ah, I see," I said. "That's fascinating...and, of course, the museum wouldn't just be a place for artifacts; it would preserve the living history of the community, stories like the ones you told just now."

"Sounds like the kind of project we'd all like to get behind, Mr. Wingfield," said the reeve.

This sounded promising. "That's wonderful. What kind of support could I expect from council?"

"We can give you an agreement in principle to the undertaking... or an undertaking that we are principally in agreement... either one."

"But I meant, would there be any chance of funding?"

The reeve handed off to Harold, the clerk.

"Your worship," sighed Harold. "I am given to understand by the restructuring committee that our funding is to be held in abeyance pending the results of negotiations on the provincial funding formulas."

The reeve turned back to me to interpret. "What Harold is saying, Mr. Wingfield, is we don't have a budget right now."

"When will you get one?"

The reeve looked back at Harold.

"Your worship," he offered patiently. "Budgets would be struck by council once it is reconstituted, and that again is attending on the ratification of the new boundaries by the Legislature."

"It's up to the province, Mr. Wingfield," explained the reeve.

"But... if you have no budget," I protested, "no jurisdiction and no constituency, why are you meeting?"

All eyebrows went up as if I had asked the silliest question in the world.

"Council's the fourth Thursday of the month," said Ernie. "Always has been."

"Now, Mr. Wingfield," said the reeve. "Had you given any thought to where this museum might be located?"

I explained to them the possibilities offered by the

abandoned mill property just down the road from the township office. "I understand the land belongs to the township. It's central and it appears to be structurally sound..."

Their silent stares brought me to a halt.

"The mill?" asked Ernie in astonishment.

"Did he say the Hollyhock Mill?" echoed Wilfrid.

"Any thought to anyplace else?" asked the reeve.

"Well, no, I thought—"

The reeve cut me off. "G'day, Mr. Wingfield. Thanks again for comin' to council. Harold, do you have the hall committee report there?"

Apparently, my audience with council was over. Obviously I'd put my foot wrong somehow, but I was at a loss to explain where. I gathered up my papers and left. Back at Freddy's, Willy and Dave pushed past me in the doorway, carrying cases of beer, followed by Spike and several other dogs. Willy set his case down and raised his hands in benediction.

"Rejoice, children, for those of ye who thirst shall be refreshed," he said.

Spike came over and put his head on my knee. I was surprised to see him. He doesn't usually wander away from the house when I'm not at home.

"What's Spike doing here?" I asked.

Willy's head popped up from behind the fridge door, where he was loading in party supplies. "Ah...we were down at your place lookin' at the Chicago price again, Uncle Walt."

Dave nodded and plunked a bottle of Labatt's 50 down in front of me. "Guess his old nose still works good enough to sniff out a party."

For many years, Maggie's absence from the community for more than twenty-four hours always served as the green light for one of "Freddy's benders." Even though Maggie no longer shares the same premises with her brother, her going away still triggers a powerful reflex response. The phone rang and Freddy answered it.

"Hyello?" he chirped, then suddenly whirled and shushed us to be quiet. He covered the receiver with his hand and whispered, "It's Maggie!" The others froze. Freddy put the phone back up to his ear. "Uh-huh," he said. "Uh-huh ... sure, we will ... you bet ... Walt? No, haven't seen Walt all day." He leaned over the counter and squinted out the window. "There's lights on at the barn. I expect he's closin' up." He winked at me and grinned. "Okay ... Okay. We'll see you then." He carefully hung up the receiver and turned to us. "She's safe and sound in Barrie ... till Monday. Gentlemen ... you may smoke!"

A little later Freddy came over to me and presented me with a handful of insulated wires. "Walt," he said. "Could you hang onto these till Monday?"

"Sure," I said. "What are these?"

"These here would be the coil wires for every internal combustion engine on the farm. It's part of our designated drinking program. If you hide 'em somewhere and don't tell us till Monday, chances are the township will be a safer place. G'day, Squire, come on in."

The Squire hobbled in the doorway and raised his eyebrows. For a moment I wasn't sure if he approved of the scene.

"G'day, fellas," he said. "My doctor tells me I'm not to do any work. So I figgered this is the place not to do it."

They all settled into couches, dogs flopped around their feet, Dave tuned up his guitar, and Freddy blew the dust out of his accordion.

"So, Walt," said Freddy. "How did your meetin' go with the Fathers of Confederation down there in Hollyhock?"

I told them that the meeting had gone quite well and the council seemed quite supportive until I mentioned the possibility of using the mill property in Hollyhock.

"The Hollyhock Mill!" said Freddy. "Is that where you were thinkin' of puttin' it? Now, Walt, you never told me that!"

"All right," I said. "Could someone please explain to me what the problem is with the Hollyhock Mill?"

"It's haunted," said Freddy.

"Haunted?" I laughed. "What nonsense is this?"

"Now, Uncle Walt," said Willy. "You don't mean to say you've been up here this long and nobody's told you the story of the Laird McNabb and the curse on the Hollyhock Mill?"

"You gotta tell 'im, Willy," said Dave.

"Okay, but I gotta have this." Willy lifted Freddy's accordion out of his lap, put one foot up on a chair and played a sombre minor chord.

"Long ago, when the land was young and men paid cash for their cars, the Laird McNabb owned all the land from Hollyhock up to the Glen. And though he was wealthy, he was a hard, hard man.

"He grew a bit of corn, and he milled a bit of flour, and he stilled a bit of gin, but the chief delight he took in life was givin' the back of his hand to the poor country folk of the township.

"One night a banshee appeared to him as he was goin' to bed and said: 'McNabb, ye've cheated the honest farmers of this township long enough and if you do not mend your ways I will smite ye like ye've never been smit before.'

"That would have been good enough for the likes of you and me. Being interviewed by a banshee in the middle of the night while standing in your underwear...that would make an angel out of some of the worst cases in the Commercial Hotel. But not the Laird McNabb.

"McNabb would have none of it. He scorned the banshee's words, so the banshee caused the corn harvest to fail and dried up the creek so the mill would not run, and still the Laird would not relent...so she sent cluster flies to torment him, and still the Laird would not relent...and finally she sent a grant application form for tile drainage with no instructions on how to fill it out, and that cracked him. The Laird dove into the millpond to drown himself and broke his neck...it bein' dried up like it was. And so the mill sits crumbling and abandoned and a curse lies on it, down to this very day."

Freddy snatched the accordion back from Willy. "That isn't anything like the curse," he snorted. "Jeez! Let the Squire tell it."

The Squire sat forward in his easy chair and waited for quiet.

"The Miller McNabb, Walt, was the man who brought out the first company of Scots settlers to the bush here. He'd been a landowner in Scotland and he lorded it over the other settlers and treated them like a bunch of serfs. He set up the mill there in Hollyhock and wouldn't let anyone in the settlement trade anywhere else. And he got rich.

He had three daughters, the prettiest girls in the Settlement, but the mother died young and it was left to the Miller McNabb to raise the girls. As the years went by, he got so he wouldn't let them out of his sight. Not for a minute. Every young lad in the township was tom-cattin' around, so McNabb told the girls they had to stay in the big stone house up by the mill.

"In spite of his efforts, these girls got to know young fellas, and they all fell in love, and one day they cornered the old man and demanded the freedom to get married. Well, the Miller McNabb flew into a rage, and he boarded up the windows, and he bricked up the doorways, and he had an iron deadbolt forged across the front door that locked with a brass key he kept on a chain around his neck."

"Good Lord!" I said. "How did he get away with this?"

"They were Presbyterians, Walt," said Freddy. "That kinda behaviour didn't exactly stand out in those days."

Squire continued. "Well, the young fellas hatched a plot to free the girls. And one night in a big storm, they surprised the Miller McNabb in the mill and knocked him out and stole the key from around his neck. They freed the girls and got in a boat tied down at the wharf below the dam and off they went. Before long, the Miller McNabb woke up, and he felt the key gone, and he ran down to the door of the house and found it standing wide open, with the key still in the lock. He looked out and saw them all floatin' off down the river. And he snatched up the key and climbed out on the dam at the height of the storm and screamed a curse at them, and then he started pulling boards out of the millrace. The water was already high and, first thing you know, the stones started falling out of the dam and the foundations around the mill wheel gave out. Then the whole works came crashing down: the dam, the mill wheel—"

"Twenty-five cats and his whole collection of moose heads off the wall—" added Willy.

"—and McNabb himself. And, last of all, the great millstone came tumbling down, and it crushed the Miller McNabb as dead as a nit in the riverbed."

"Yep," giggled Willy. "And the place has been known ever since as 'Miller Flats.'"

The Squire sighed and carried on. "The river flowed over its banks for three days and three nights. And when the flood was over they searched the river for the girls and the young fellas and the Miller McNabb, but none of them were never found.

"And six men stood in the river and lifted with all their strength and they tried to raise the stone. They all felt a tremor pass through it. Like a live thing, it was. And they let it fall back, and they all ran away. And that stone has never been moved from that day to this."

"I guess everybody figured if it could move itself, why bother?" said Willy.

"Laugh if you want, Willy," said Freddy. "But of those six men, not one lived more than a year after that night."

"Of course they didn't. With the boss gone and nobody to tell them what to do, they drank themselves to death in the Hillsdale Hotel."

I agreed that this was quite a story, but I pointed out that the problem with the museum site wasn't the mill itself. It was the millstone. That's the thing people won't touch.

"I don't know, Walt," said the Squire. "Folks are pretty spooked about the whole place."

"But," I persisted, "if people could be shown there's nothing wrong with moving the millstone, all their objections to the site would just fade away, wouldn't they?"

The Squire shrugged. "Well, that makes sense, but—"

"And don't you see, the story makes it even better as a museum site." I turned to the others. "That's the real living history of the community."

Freddy shook his head. "Some history is better forgotten, Walt. That stone is cursed, I tell you, and anyone who touches it will come to a bad end."

Dave nodded. "Uncle Freddy has a point. You know, Sparky McEwen went fishin' there once and sat on that stone by accident. And he sure has had a run of bad luck."

"Why? What happened to him?" I asked.

"He didn't get his property tax rebate this year, and his kids have all moved back home."

"Look, I'll move the stone myself. Nobody else needs to be involved. Then, when people see I'm not cursed... end of problem."

Freddy was unconvinced. "You may not be the right guy for this, Walt."

"What do you mean?"

The Squire patted my hand. "What Freddy's sayin' is, the way you do stuff around here, it's hard to tell if you're in the grip of a deadly curse or just having a normal day."

Yours sincerely,
Walt

June 10

Dear Ed,

I haven't found any historical record of the Miller McNabb, but that doesn't prove much. It seems most of the early history here is in dispute. For instance, most accounts say the opening of the road from the Town of York started the flow of goods and people that really established the community. But I found this entry in a local history book— Dr. D.J. Goulding's *With Axe and Flask: The History of Persephone Township from Pre-Cambrian Times to the Present*:

> *Reaching Larkspur under any conditions was a difficult and hazardous journey and could take many days. But building a road made the situation even worse because as soon as it was finished 39 taverns sprang up over a distance of 38 miles. Some people never made it to Larkspur at all. It wasn't until Prohibition in 1916 that people discovered you could make the trip in an hour and a half.*

I had a small success with poultry my first year here. My two geese, Colonel Belknap and General Longstreet, grew to fourteen pounds each and fetched a dollar a pound. Modest, but an encouraging start, you'll agree. But it's like those guys in the midway who let you win a couple of times to get you hooked. Then they take all your money. I was out at the mailbox last week in another one of those impromptu neighbourhood roadside meetings, this time with no less than four vehicles blocking the Seventh Line. I was driving back from the Coop in Demeter Centre with a flyer advertising day-old meat chicks from a Mennonite supplier in Elmira. I was hesitating because of the terrible luck I have had with whatever birds I try—ducks, chickens, turkeys, guinea hens, you name it. The guys were all sympathetic.

"You've buried a lot of birds here, Walt," said the Squire.

"Yeah," said Don. "You may as well call it a poultry farm, Walt. That's pretty much what the ground's made of now."

"It's not your fault," said the Squire. "All you have to do is look at a chicken and you can tell they were not meant to live. Everything loves to kill a chicken."

Freddy looked at the flyer. "You know, if you're thinking of going into these meat chickens, what you should do is, when you pick 'em up from the hatchery, set a flat of them on the front seat beside you and fire one at every mailbox you see on the way home. You try it, Walt, it'll make you feel better in the long run."

I read an article last year, from an organic gardening magazine, about an experiment at an apple orchard in Washington State where they were raising free-range chickens to help break the cycle of bugs coming up out of the ground and into the fruit. It sounded like a terrific idea, so I mailed away for fifty Dominique chickens, which are a rare American breed that the poultry catalogue described as independent, good foragers and "a pretty good meat bird." Then I released thousands of beneficial bugs— ladybugs, lacewings and tricogramma wasps—natural predators of apple pests.

I was trying to work in harmony with the natural world, but it turns out that the natural world is a pretty violent place. As Freddy says, "Nature's a lot like Revenue

Canada. She sets her own rules and she doesn't always tell you what they are."

The chickens ate all the beneficial bugs; dogs ate the chickens. By the end of the summer it was dogs: 37; chickens: 0. In the fall, hunters snuck in and ate all the apples, and the natural cycle was complete.

I did manage to put seven chickens in the freezer in December. At seven months they weighed four and a half pounds each. We had one for dinner just before Christmas. It was the toughest chicken I have ever eaten in my life. It tasted like it had run all the way from Washington State. Maggie pointed out that these were the fastest ones out of fifty chickens, so what did I expect?

That left me with five hens and one rooster—with a very bad twitch. The rooster started attacking me, so I decided to teach him a lesson. Every time he came at me I whacked him over the head with a leather glove. I did this thirty-five times before I realized that a rooster's head is designed the way it is for a purpose. It is meant to hold a certain amount of inherited information but it will not accept new information. There is no room in that head for a new thought. So all you can do is take the head off, I guess.

I finally moved the survivors into protective custody in the henhouse for the winter, but even there they weren't safe. A couple of months ago, I came out and found that a raccoon had broken through the chicken wire covering the window in the middle of the night and killed three of the hens. I asked Maggie if there was anything you can do about a raccoon.

"Yes," she said. "You get one of those humane traps— it's called a Havahart Trap—and you trap the 'coon in the humane trap. Then you beat it to death with a shovel."

So the score started to even up a bit. But then I found that raccoons are a lot like taxicabs at the airport. You take one out and another one moves in to take its place. It's a lot of work burying a raccoon. Some of them weigh twenty-five pounds, and it can really put a dent in your morning schedule. But I've found you can drop them out at the highway and the Ministry crews will pick them up. Just don't drop them in the same place every time.

I'm down to my last chicken now. There were two, but this morning I opened the door of the henhouse too quickly, and one of them fell over with a stroke. Couldn't take the pressure, I guess. The Squire helped me bury it this afternoon.

"I'm beginning to see why this breed got so rare, Walt. They seem to prefer extinction."

I patted the shovel on the loose dirt and straightened up to find the Squire studying the hill across the road.

"My oh my," he said. "Where did that come from?"

I wasn't sure what he was looking at. "Look at that," he said, waving a finger at the view that stretched away to the east. Over the past week, with the warm weather, the trees were just now bursting into their full summer plumage. "Here, put your shovel down and look there. Fourteen shades of green, full of birds and bugs. Smells better than a bakery. If a fella can't take pleasure in a sight like that, he should go down to the real estate office and slap a sign on her today."

"It's nice, isn't it?" I agreed.

"And look at the way the old forest has come back on Calvin Currie's hill pasture."

I hesitated. There were a few cedars in the gullies on the side of the hill, but, for the most part, the field was grown up in dogwood and thistles.

"Forest?" I said.

"Yeah, look. There's maple up there and beech... there's even a stand of pin oaks. Come on, Walt, let's take a walk up through it..."

He took a step forward and then stopped. He blinked and frowned and looked back at me. After a moment he said, "You don't see it, do you?"

"No," I said carefully, taking his arm. "But you do. You remember it from a long time ago. Come on, I'll help you home."

We walked slowly back out to the lane and down to the mailbox. At the road, we stood together in the cool evening air, listening to barn sounds down at Don's. A gravel truck chugged up the town line in the distance. Two groundhogs chased each other through the ditch and out onto the hayfield.

"Are you all right from here?" I asked gently.

He smiled and patted my shoulder. "You're very kind to an old man, Walt. You have a way about you. I don't know what's the matter with me. There's never been a stand of pin oaks on Calvin's hill."

I watched him hobble back down his lane until he climbed up the steps of his verandah and the old screen door banged behind him.

Yours sincerely,
Walt

June 21

Dear Ed,

I was on my way out this morning when I met Willy and Dave at the kitchen doorway. I could tell from the look on their faces that something was up.

"Say, Uncle Walt," said Willy. "Do you got a minute? Me and Dave's got a little problem and we were thinkin' maybe you could help. You know that Dr. Winegard that bought the cattle with us? We just got a call from him. Revenue Canada is askin' him and his friends a bunch of questions, and there's a coupla government guys comin' up today to look at these cattle."

"Ah," I said. "An audit. That's not unusual."

"But they're not just looking at Dr. Winegard's books. They're doin' a bunch of his dentist friends, too."

Dave threw up his hands. "Like what kind of shady characters are these dentists, anyway?"

"Look," I said. "There's nothing to worry about. They're not auditing you. Just be polite and show them you have nothing to hide. You might take them to lunch at the Red Hen."

Willy scratched his neck. "Now there's a good idea," he said. "We're gonna be kinda busy. Could you take them to lunch for us? Like, you know how to talk to these people."

I don't know why, but I said yes. They asked me to be sure to put the visitors in the corner booth by the kitchen. By the time it occurred to me to ask why, they were gone. I met the audit team in the Red Hen restaurant at twelve o'clock. A man and a woman, carrying clipboards and a map of the township. I rose and introduced myself.

"So," I asked. "Are you all done?"

"Done?" said the young man. "No, no. We saw one herd this morning. We have more this afternoon, don't we?"

"Yes," said his partner. "There's another herd on the Second Line ... that must be the other side of Larkspur."

I waved at Donna, the waitress, and she came over to take our orders. While we were sitting there, chatting, a movement at the window caught my eye. A cow's head appeared. The next moment it bobbed its head and disappeared. Another cow appeared. I did a double take and realized the whole street behind was obscured by the backs of moving cattle. I went quickly over to the window and closed the blinds.

"Gosh, that sun's hot. I thought I'd close the blinds," I said, grinning like an idiot. I snuck a peek out through the slats and caught a glimpse of Dave on horseback at the back of the herd, hat waving high above his head. I heard a distant "Yipee-i-o-kiyay!"

"What was that?" said the auditor.

"Oh," I said. "That was me. I said, 'The pudding's tapioca today.' Will you try some? Say, Donna, could you turn up that radio? That's my favourite song, don't you love it? What's it called, Donna?"

Donna stopped chewing for a moment, shifted her quid to the other side of her mouth and said, "'I Used to Kiss Her on the Lips but I Left Her Behind for You.'"

At four o'clock, I was back on my verandah trying to make sense of the whole situation with Don.

"I feel like they were using me as a decoy," I said. "They must have been trying to make the auditors think they have more cattle than they actually do. The question is, how many more, and why?"

Don nodded. "Mm-hmm. Pinning those boys down is like trying to put six cats in a basket. When they get here, we'll just turn them upside down and shake."

A few minutes later the boys drove in, grinning like schoolboys on the last day of class.

"Good news, Uncle Walt," said Willy. "The revenooers figger they hit a dry hole. They're headin' south."

"Is that right?" I said. "I want to see both of you...in my office. Come on, Don."

They filed in meekly and sat down on the couch beside the computer. Don and I drew up two chairs and sat facing them.

"Now," I said. "How many cattle do you boys have?"

"Let's see," Willy said, stroking his chin and studying the ceiling. "On the home place there'd be..."

"Never mind that stuff," interrupted Don. "We want a number. Now."

Willy swallowed, looked at Dave and looked back at us. "A hundred and twenty-five."

"All right," said Don. "Who do they belong to?"

"I guess, like, originally...Dr. Winegard."

"You guess. Now what cattle were those auditors looking for?"

"I don't know. Maybe...the other ones? Ya see, Dr. Winegard got nine of his dentist friends to send us a hundred thousand dollars each to buy cattle. Well, we got no place to put that many cattle. What were we supposed to do?"

"Normally, you give the money back," said Don.

Willy and Dave looked at each other in surprise. "Jeez," said Willy. "We never thought of that. Anyway we bought a contract for feeder cattle on the Chicago futures market."

"But how did you do that?" I asked.

"On your computer, Uncle Walt."

"But you can't do that. You can't speculate in that market without a licence. The machine won't let you make a transaction unless you use my password—"

"Spike," said Dave. "It wasn't that hard, Uncle Walt. We got it on the third try."

I got a sinking feeling in the pit of my stomach. "Omigosh," I said. "You bought nine hundred thousand dollars worth of cattle futures under my name?"

"Jeez no," said Willy. "It was a lot more than that. We put the whole wad in your margin account. All you need is five percent down. You can tie up a lot of cattle that way. Hey, Dave. What did we figger nine hundred thousand got us?"

Dave tapped on the calculator on my desk. "Let's see, if five percent is nine hundred thousand, then a hundred percent would be . . . is it this button here?"

I snatched up the calculator and punched in the numbers. Eighteen million dollars. I put a hand over my eyes and waited for my head to clear.

"What's the price of cattle been doing since you bought this contract?" I asked finally.

"Gone down like a stone," said Dave brightly. "Nearly twenty cents."

"So, in three months' time, if the price doesn't recover, you will both be on the hook for two point four million dollars. What did you plan to do then?"

"We thought the responsible thing to do would be to make a run for the border. Unless you got some ideas, Uncle Walt. You do have some ideas, don't you?"

"Yes, I certainly do. I call the Securities Commission. Then I call the fraud squad."

The boys shrank back in horror. Don put his hand on my arm.

"You can't do that to them, Walt," he said solemnly.

"Why not, may I ask?"

"They aren't employees. They're your kin."

I looked out the open window as a bumblebee bumped against the screen, dropped to the sill, crawled up and dropped again. Don finally broke the silence.

"Can you get them out of it?"

"I don't know," I muttered. "Maybe. We'll have to dump the whole business right now."

"But who's goin' to touch it?" asked Dave.

"As it stands right now...nobody. We'll have to make it more attractive. What I can do is put together a butterfly spread." They all looked at me blankly. "You know, a hedge contract based on a matrix of contradictory speculative outcomes."

Willy nodded hopefully. "Oh, yeah. One of those..."

"Say you're deciding what to plant," I explained as patiently as I could. "The variables are temperature and rainfall. For hot and wet you plant rice...for hot and dry...cactus, I guess. For cold and wet...mushrooms. For cold and dry..."

"Martinis?" offered Willy.

"Whatever. If you plant all four crops: rice, cactus, mushrooms and juniper, one of them is certain to be a winner. So, we have to build an investment model that works the same way, only for cattle futures. Now...let's see what's out there."

I leaned over the computer and tapped into the Chicago market. Over the next half hour we took large positions in cattle in three corners of the planet. For me it was like going back in time...to twenty years ago on the commodities desk at McFeeters, Bartlett & Hendrie. The difference was, in those days I didn't know any better. And my nerves were a lot younger.

Willy looked over my shoulder at the screen. "What's that number there, Uncle Walt?"

"At this precise moment, that is our total liability."

Willy whistled softly. "Hokey jeez, I thought it was your social insurance number."

"All right," I said. "Now...we fold the whole thing together and put a 'For Sale' sign on it."

"You're not getting' yourself into trouble on account of us, are you, Uncle Walt?" asked Willy. "Maggie would drown us in a sack like a couple of kittens."

Dave agreed. "She'd stake us out on an anthill—"

There was a beep and I looked back at the screen. An offer was coming up now. A very reasonable offer, it seemed to me.

"See there?" I said. "I can get you out of the contract for that figure."

Dave worked the calculator furiously. "I guess if we sell the cattle we got now, we could just pay the dentists back. But then we'll have worked all summer for nothin'."

"So what?" said Willy. "We worked last summer for nothin', too. Go ahead and sell it, Uncle Walt."

I put one finger up in the air. "There's one condition. Neither of you ever touch this machine again without me in this room. Is that clear?"

They both crossed their hearts and spit. I clicked the mouse on the "confirm sale" button and waited. The machine burbled for sixty seconds and a confirmation code finally appeared on the screen. I accepted it and the sale was complete.

"Done," I sighed.

"So...who bought it, Walt?" asked Don.

I looked at the bottom of the screen. "It says, The Christian Democratic Front for Peaceful Change of San Carlo de...Holy smoke, it's that new military junta in South America. We'd better do the paperwork on this right away. They have anthills, too."

Yours sincerely,
Walt

July 7

Dear Ed,

This morning, I decided to move the millstone. I've learned a bit about this kind of civil engineering over the past few years. Nothing beats a team of horses for moving something heavy and awkward up a slope that's too steep for conventional machinery. Last year, I won Don's grudging admiration when I managed to get Feedbin and Mortgage to haul a load of cedar posts out of the swamp. Since then I've refined the technique by putting King in the middle. He acts as a kind of chaperone to the ladies, keeping them from having too much fun. I even had a set of heavy harness made up to accommodate the three of them. I pulled a length of heavy logging chain out of the shed and we set off down the Centre Road in the direction of Hollyhock.

The village was its usual idyllic self. Some kids with their parents were at the playground by the bridge. There were several cars parked and some fishermen on the bridge itself. I waved to them as I steered the horses off the road and we made our way down the steep embankment. The fishermen waved back. When we got to the riverbank, I tied the horses to a cedar branch.

The millstone lay, as I'd seen it before, half-submerged on a gravel bed below the ruined millrace, creating a little V-shaped eddy in the water. I waded out through the steady current with the logging chain and studied this fabled piece of masonry. It was a fairly ordinary millstone: about four feet across and maybe ten inches thick. Standing this close, I could see it wasn't lying flat; it was wedged into the gravel and on the high side there was a cavity of about six inches underneath. It occurred to me that it would be possible to haul this thing out of the river without actually touching it. Not that it made any difference, of course. I bent down and put my hand in the cold water, gingerly reaching towards the millstone.

"FFFFDDDDDDD!" said Feedbin from the riverbank. It gave me a start. I looked up and down the river and found no hazards in sight. A small crowd had gathered on the bridge. They appeared to be watching me. I dropped the hook end of the chain through the hole in the stone and reached into the water again to pull it through the other side. Something moved against my hand and I jerked it out again, almost losing my balance in the current. A crayfish shot out from under the stone.

I looked up at the line of faces on the bridge. "Crayfish," I called to them and smiled. I picked up the hook again and fastened it snugly back on the chain. Then I waded out of the stream to the horses, who were now staring at me.

"I didn't touch it," I promised. "No hands."

I untied them, backed them gently into the water and hooked up the chain. Now, using King as an anchor horse in tricky pulls like this has always made the kind of difference that an insurance company would really appreciate. Without him, as the poet says, "things fall apart; the centre cannot hold." With him, we have two speeds: dead slow and stop.

I gathered up the lines and clucked softly. The horses stepped forward, the chain snapped up out of the water, the stone slid a few inches sideways and disappeared under the surface. The crowd at the bridge watched intently. The millstone slid a few more feet, bounced gently against a stone and emerged at the water's edge.

"Okay, you guys...but slowly now...Giddyup!"

We started up the bank. Suddenly I felt that old familiar tremor pass through the horses. Feedbin started cantering on the spot, Mortgage stood up on her hind legs, ears flat, eyes staring wildly. I fought to control them. King held his ground. Thank heavens for King. Then, suddenly, King lost his mind. He took a gigantic leap forward, then another and another. I tumbled back, tripped over the chain and found myself face to face with the millstone, careering up the hill. I had two choices: either hang onto the chain or find out first hand what the Miller McNabb had discovered about meeting the millstone at high speed. I decided to hang on, and an awesome force hauled me up the slope. My grip loosened and I slid down the chain until my feet were touching the millstone. The horses gained the crest of the hill, scrambled sideways and stopped, snorting and trembling. The millstone and I bounced along the face of the bluff, then swung out into empty space.

"Whooaa...whooaaa..." I prayed. The horses stood together, trembling above me. "This is okay," I thought. If they would just stay put. "Whoa there, horsies. For once in your pea-brained lives, please just stay whooaaed."

I'd swung out into a gorge where the embankment had eroded. The drop beneath me wasn't all the way to the river; only about halfway, but still far enough. King was calming down. I could see figures racing off the bridge. Help was on its way. If the horses stayed still and the harness held, everything would be all right.

It was good harness. The fittings were brass; the tugs were made of triple-laminated horsehide. Mennonites had sewn it all together by hand. They were good fellows, those Mennonites. They use that tough, sinewy, white thread...I looked up and saw some of that stupid, flimsy, white thread going pip!...pip!

At the hospital they took X-rays and put me in a bed for observation. When I woke up, Maggie and Freddy were standing at my bedside.

"You made the papers this time, Walt," said Freddy.

"Thanks for coming, both of you," I croaked.

Maggie shook her head. "I just seem to go from hospital to hospital these days. How's your head, dear?"

"Oh, I'm fine. I just got a bit of a bump."

"A bump?" said Freddy. "Walt, when you came around you made a speech thanking the rescue party for coming out to the annual meeting."

Maggie leaned forward and looked me squarely in the eye. "Are you well enough to tell me just what you thought you were doing down there at the mill?"

"I just wanted to show people there's nothing wrong with it as a museum site. They've got this notion that the millstone's cursed. I suppose you know all about it."

"Of course I've heard of it!" she exclaimed. "It's the excuse you hear whenever someone suggests cleaning up the trash in that river. I guess there's a few cursed washing machines and bedsteads down there, too. Walt, do you think you might give this museum idea a bit of a rest?"

"You think I'm being obsessive? It's just that it's a good idea, and it seems a shame we can't do it as long as people have this cockeyed notion of a curse."

Freddy looked at the ceiling and cleared his throat. "You may have dug yourself in deeper there, Walt. The newspaper story says a couple of the eyewitnesses claim they saw the Miller McNabb riding King up that bank, in a black robe, with no head."

"What? Oh, wonderful! But, wait a minute. If the rider had no head, how could they tell it was . . . oh, never mind."

Yours sincerely,
Walt

July 15

Dear Ed,

Last night Maggie and I were finishing up the dishes when the house shuddered. We both went to the window and looked out. The wind was up, but the sky was clear and the moon shone down on the fields. It all looked peaceful enough to me.

"There's water in her eye," said Maggie ominously.

"There's what?"

"The moon. You can tell there's a blow coming in. Are the barn doors shut?"

I looked again at the moon. There was a ring of vapoury blue light around it. I checked the wall barometers we got for our wedding. They all said "fair and dry."

"Never mind those things, Walt. Look at the moon. Did you latch the barn doors shut?"

By now I know that voice. I stepped out onto the verandah. The wind was up, all right. It whipped the screen door out of my hands and banged it shut behind me. I closed up the tool shed and the henhouse, then dashed over to the barn and pushed the big sliding door shut. I always get a surge of energy, battening down for a storm. When I'm done I like to stand for a minute on the gangway and marvel at the power of the elements. It's exhilarating to see the clouds tumble across the night sky and the wind make the young oak trees bend double and flap furiously.

Actually, I'd never seen them do that before. The sky certainly was an odd colour, too. Then, I heard a loud bang and looked over to see that the door of the henhouse had blown open. There was only one hen left, but I didn't want to lose the door. The henhouse was straight upwind, and it took me a few moments to get there. When I did, the door was flapping hard against the wall. It took everything I had to bring it around into the wind and close it.

A pail flew by. I guess the tool shed was open again. I jogged over to check on it. More stuff was blowing by me, including some pretty big wooden boards. Something soft bounced off my shoulder. It was the hen, headed east, out of control. I looked back and saw that the henhouse had disappeared. Then Maggie was there beside me. She was speaking, but I could barely hear her voice over the roar of the wind.

"Come to the house, Walt. NOW!"

Then the rain hit. We ran over to the house. In the shelter of the verandah, we looked back towards the barn. A flash of lightning revealed it for a moment, just long enough for us to see a section of steel roof curling up to the peak like an orange peel.

"There's nothing we can do," said Maggie. "Come inside."

We lay in bed in our bedroom off the kitchen, listening to the storm hammer the house. When a gust of wind hit, the whole house would lean and creak and go "whub-a-whub-a-whub." Then the wind dropped and it lurched back again.

"You don't suppose there's the slightest chance of the house blowing over, do you?" I asked.

Maggie looked around at the room. "If it does," she said, "this window will be on the floor, the floor will be that wall there, and the wood stove will come through," she glanced at the ceiling, "about here." We went down to the basement and spent the rest of the night on the sofa bed.

Next morning we went out to look at the damage. All the steel had blown off the south half of the barn roof and the boards were all blown out of the gable end. The big sliding door had disappeared. The tool shed was gone, the henhouse was gone and the yard was littered with debris.

"What a mess," sighed Maggie. "I'd better get down to the shop and see what the damage is in town."

As she drove off, the Squire appeared, carrying my hen.

"Found this bird on my verandah," he said, handing her to me. "I think she's about due for a therapist. And, say, is that your barn door floating in my pond?"

"In your pond? Good heavens. So, what's the damage at your place?"

"No damage. Why, did you get a bit of wind last night?"

"A bit of wind?" I snorted. "More like a hurricane! Look at the place."

"That's funny," he said. "I didn't notice anything. I had coffee with Freddy and Don this morning. They didn't talk about any storm."

We went back to the kitchen, where I made a few calls and verified that no one else on the Seventh Line was aware of a windstorm last night. I looked at the Squire.

"This is weird. I know isolated windstorms happen, but do you think there might be something to this curse thing, after all?"

The Squire sat down at the kitchen table and took a big breath.

"Did I ever tell you about John Hand?" he asked. I shook my head. "John Hand had a great team of bloods, and he was very proud of them. They must have been the nicest looking team of horses in the county. John would spend extra time with them, feedin' them up and brushin' them till their coats shone. He loved them horses. On Sundays, if the weather was bad, he'd stay home from church rather than leave the team in an open shed. Well, one night in the fall, John Hand's barn burned to the ground. He lost all his stock, maybe twelve heifer cows and the same number of calves, all the year's hay and grain and that beautiful team of bloods.

"Folks pitched in, and we got John through the winter, and in the spring we helped him build again. I wasn't much more than a kid then, but I helped too; I just got into the habit of walkin' up there when I could and I'd put in an afternoon with him. One day we were workin' on a fence and John turns to me and says, 'I know why that barn burned.' I thought he meant someone had set the fire on purpose and I didn't know what to say. And then John says, 'I was worshipping horse flesh instead of the Lord.'"

"Wait a minute," I said. "He thought God burned his barn down?"

The Squire nodded. "That's what he thought."

"And is that what you think?"

The Squire sighed. "Well, I don't know. But John Hand was the only man I ever knew who would smoke in a barn. Myself, I think God kept that barn standing as long as He could and it was John who burned it down."

"So, what you're saying is that I should look for an ordinary explanation for all of this?"

The Squire did not reply.

"I'm going back to the mill and figure out what really made the horses bolt. Enough of this nonsense."

"In that case, I'd better go with you. Maggie asked me to keep an eye on you."

The Squire drove me down the Centre Road to Hollyhock. We parked by the mill and walked over to the edge of the bank. The millstone lay below us, halfway down the slope, caught in a cleft made by two birch saplings. We helped each other down the embankment, noticing the skid marks the stone had made on its way up the slope. Near the bottom, I saw the first deep gouges in the clay that showed where the horses got excited. I pointed to them.

"It was right about here that King went nuts. But I don't see anything." Something moved on the ground and made me jump.

"What is it, Walt?" asked the Squire.

We both looked closer. There was a rustle in a clump of dead cedar twigs and a big fat toad climbed out and blinked at us. I guess he was sleeping.

"That explains it, then," said the Squire.

"It does?"

"It made you jump, didn't it? A horse can't stand that sort of thing. Makes him think the ground is moving."

"Really? Well, so much for the curse, eh? Do you suppose if I kissed him he would turn into the Miller McNabb?"

We followed Mr. Toad as he hopped down the bank towards the river. I looked out into the river to the spot where the millstone had been and saw a glint of sunlight reflect off something under the water. Something shiny. I waded out and took a closer look. It was a clover-shaped piece of metal, half buried in the gravel. I reached in and pulled out an old brass key.

"Well, I'll be . . ." I marvelled.

"Walt! Can you come here a minute?"

"Look what I found," I said, holding up the key.

"Walter! Come here . . . NOW!"

I jogged over to him quickly to see what was the matter.

"Are you all right?" I asked.

It made hardly a sound. I'd never have heard it from down by the water. Just a faint crack of wood, like a twig snapping. By the time I looked up, the millstone was flipping through the air like a huge coin in slow motion. It smashed into the riverbed right where I'd been standing and broke into three pieces.

Neither of us said anything for a long moment. Finally, the Squire said, "I reckon that'll be easier to move now."

I stared at him in amazement. "You knew that was going to happen, didn't you?"

The Squire shut his eyes and nodded. "Yeah, I did. I saw it. A couple of days ago. At the time I didn't know when it was happening. Not till I seen you standing there."

"So these things you've been seeing, some of them, they are real. They just haven't happened yet."

"Maybe they've happened a lot of times, Walt. Just not to us."

"You saved my life."

The Squire nodded again. He looked frail and frightened. "Can we go home now?" he asked.

We hear a lot these days about the Internet, as if it were some kind of new development. We've had it in Persephone Township for many years. Only we call it "the party line." Of course, it's more efficient than the Internet, because instead of "logging on" for hours in the hope of finding something interesting, with the party line you just have to memorize the individualized ring of whomever it is you want to eavesdrop on.

Another superior feature is that, with practice, you can tell approximately how many other eavesdroppers there are, because with a party line the more phones that are off the hook, the less current goes to each phone and the harder it is to hear. When the Squire and I got back to his place, I phoned Maggie at the store.

"He saved my life, Maggie. It's the most amazing thing!"

"That's nice, Walt. I'll see you at home, dear."

"But, Maggie, don't you see, he knew it was going to happen because he'd already seen it. You understand? These things he's been seeing—some of them—are in the future!"

Maggie's voice was fainter now. "That's fine, dear. Bye-bye now."

"I beg your pardon?"

"I said that's fine, Walt. Bye now."

"I can hardly hear you, Maggie . . ."

"Just a minute, Walt. THIS IS A PRIVATE CONVER-SATION. COULD YOU ALL PLEASE HANG UP!"

There was a series of clicks and Maggie's voice came up loud and clear again.

"We can talk about this at home, dear. Now hang up."

The Squire sighed. "I'd kinda hoped this coulda been our little secret, Walt."

"Oh. Sorry."

Yours sincerely,
Walt

July 21

Dear Ed,

Next morning Spike and I rose with the sun and went down to do chores. At this time of year, with everyone out on pasture, there aren't many chores to do. I just put out some feed for the chicken and there's one cow, Cupcakes, to milk. Instead of chasing her up to the barn, I decided to take the pail down to her under an apple tree by the pond. I sat down in the grass beside her and milked her out while she chewed and burped. The sun was beginning to warm my face through the morning mist. A gentle breeze rustled the leaves, bringing the fencerows to life.

"How are you now, Walt?"

It was the Squire. "I feel great, thanks," I grinned. "You're up early."

"Yeah, it's too nice to stay in. This is the kind of morning it's fun to be a farmer. Makes everything look special. Well, how about that! Look there."

I rose quickly. "Good Lord, what do you see now?"

But when I looked, I saw it, too. The little field beside the pond had turned snow white overnight. It was supposed to be a hayfield, but now it was thick with blooms of buckwheat. I hadn't planted buckwheat there. Last year it was a plot of corn and everybody laughed because I decided to harvest the corn myself by hand. Actually, the four pigs kept me company. They ate while I picked, and by Thanksgiving there was enough shelled corn in the barn to last Cupcakes all winter and the pigs weighed two hundred pounds. The field was a mess, so I just ran the disks over it last fall and scattered hayseed early this spring. But the Squire had an explanation.

"Old Fisher must have had buckwheat there sometime, years ago. The seed's been lyin' in the field all this time and, what with the pigs rootin' and the corn husks rottin', it was just the right conditions for nature to hand you a little surprise."

"That makes sense," I said. "I've had my weight on the

wrong foot about this museum thing, haven't I? I've been afraid of surprises, afraid of things changing. I mean, it's good to honour the past, but you can't gather it into your lap and hang on to it."

The Squire nodded. "That's what the Miller McNabb tried to do."

"And that's the real curse, isn't it? Life goes on...things change. And the change isn't always bad. It could be a field of buckwheat or a stand of pin oaks on Calvin Currie's hill. They'll be there sooner or later, won't they?"

The old man grinned at me and poked me in the shoulder. "Be there sooner if you plant 'em, Walt."

That evening after supper, Maggie and I drove down to the Orange Hall in Larkspur for the Berry Festival Dance. The Price Family Orchestra was once quite large, but over the years it has dwindled in size and repertoire. They're down to three members and four tunes.

Maggie twirled over to me in her blue dress. "Come on, Walt," she coaxed. "They're playing our song. Let's waltz."

"'When You and I Were Young,' Maggie? That's not a waltz."

"It is the way *they* play it."

We danced around the hall. Maggie sang into my ear, and suddenly there were just two people in the world, floating on a gentle river of creaky violin music and thumping piano chords.

I wandered today to the hill, Walter,
To watch the scene below.
The creek and the creaking old mill, Walter,
As we used to long ago.

Then it was my turn:

The green grove is gone from the hill, Maggie,
Where first the daisies sprung.
The creaking old mill is still, Maggie,
Since you and I were young.

Maggie stopped suddenly, as if she'd forgotten a casserole in the oven at home.

"Oh, dear," she said. "Excuse me, Walt. I'll be right back."

"What's the matter? Is something...?"

But she was gone. The Squire walked by me, followed closely by Willy. The Squire looked irritated.

"Willy, quit buggin' me!" he snarled.

"Aw, c'mon, Squire," pleaded Willy. "Next Wednesday. Demeter Downs Raceway. Our guest. You look over the racing form and, no pressure, we'll just see what comes to you."

The Squire waved him away. "It doesn't work like that. I can't turn it on and off like a light bulb."

"Okay, okay," said Willy. "Tell you what. We try Chicago again; it's perfect...we do the cattle, you do the futures."

The Squire stopped and touched his forehead. "Something's comin' to me now...flashing red lights. Cruisers. Bars on windows. G'day, Freddy...Don."

"Mrs. Lynch wants you to have a look at her bingo card, Squire," said Don solemnly.

"And when you're done there, could you have a peek at my Pick Six numbers for the Nevada?" said Freddy.

"No, I couldn't! Now back off, all of yas!"

The band struck up "The Crooked Stovepipe" and Freddy grabbed the microphone. The hall divided itself magically into groups of eight, and Freddy launched into one of his convoluted square dance calls.

"Ladies and Gentlemen," he announced. "This here's called 'Wingfield in the Straw.'"

Four hands up, and away we go
Around the hall with a do-see-do
Walt quit the job and bought some land
A hundred acres of rocks and sand.

The rooster goes out, and the hen goes in
The coons are killin' those chickens again
Three hands round, the fourth is free
So Walt and Maggie are at the K.F.C.

Grand Chain!

First couple off, second fills the void,
Walt needed a ram, so he bought Pink Floyd
Third couple off, let 'em all pass
Floyd turned out to be a pain in the ...

"How are you doin' down there?"

Form a star with a right-hand cross.
King did a bolt and gave Walt the toss.
Swing her the half, and give her heck
And Walt had a millstone round his neck.

When the dust settled, Mrs. Price brought us back full circle to the comparative calm of "When You and I Were Young." I found myself in a group with Freddy, Don and the Squire. The Squire raised his glass to me in a salute.

"Lovely evening, Walt. The kind you'll tell your children about."

"My children? Have you seen something?"

"Now, don't you start, Walt. You don't have to be Isaiah to see it. That healthy glow..."

"Yep," Don agreed. "And that smug look they get..."

Freddy nodded. "And when they plugged in the coffee urn back there, she ran outside and threw up."

Maggie appeared again in the half door of the kitchen. I excused myself and trotted over to her.

"Are you all right?" I asked.

"Just fine, Walt. Where were we?"

"'And now we are aged and grey.' Maggie...?" She took my hand and put her cheek next to mine. "Did you have anything you wanted to tell me?" I asked.

"I was waiting for the test results to make it official," she whispered. "But it seems the only people who don't know are the doctor... and you."

"Well..." I said. "Surprise, surprise!"

"Imagine, at our age. Are you pleased?"

I held her closer and sang softly in her ear:

But to me you are fair as the day, Maggie,
When you and I were young.

Yours sincerely,
Walt

A note from the editor:

So that's the way it went. Dr. Winegard and his friends got their money back from the cattle venture and sank the whole wad into the mill property. They turned it into a restaurant called the Brass Key. The story of the Miller McNabb is printed on the placemats, and the key hangs in a glass case over the fireplace. Some say the curse is broken, but I don't know. A week after the opening, the chef quit and they had to bring in Donna from the Red Hen. She fought with the cappuccino machine for three days, then she threw it out the back door over the waterfall. It lies on its side in midstream at the bottom, and nobody will touch it.

The Seventh Line wanted to hold a barn-raising for Walt and Maggie, but you need good weather for that sort of thing. So they asked the Squire to pick the day. He went into a room by himself and shut the door. When he didn't come out, they got worried and peeked in. It looked like he'd gone into some kind of trance. Turned out he was on the phone, on hold with the Environment Canada weather office. Anyway, they picked August the 10th, and it turned out perfect.

It was quite a sight. Men swarmed over the rafters like bees on a honeycomb. Willy and Dave scrambled up to the very top, nailed the ridgepole beam into place, then stood up on it, balancing beer bottles on their foreheads, making the girls scream. Maggie handed out hard hats to the ground crew. By the end of the day, it was done, and they christened it with a barn dance that very night, with the Price Family Orchestra.

Maggie and Walt want to name the baby after the Squire . . . if it's a boy . . . but it turns out the Squire's real name is Baxter Fortescue. At school, the kids used to call him Back Forty. Anyway, if it's a girl, they think they might call her Hope.

Oh, and there's more surprises all the time. We just got word on the radio news that the new military junta in South America has collapsed in bankruptcy. No details yet, but authorities credit a brilliant but mysterious financial force known only as Spike.

ON ICE

After a lot of ups and downs, Walt was riding a wave now. He and Maggie had bread on the table and a bun in the oven. But no sooner had he accepted the idea that change was not necessarily fatal to his beloved Persephone, than another, more serious issue reared its head.

If a dog bites a man, it's not news; if a man bites a dog, *that*'s news. At least that's what they say in the newspaper business. But if you run a small-town weekly it's not that simple. You have to be circumspect. Let me offer a case in point from today's paper:

> *"Once again, the Humane Society was summoned after an encounter between J. Roberts of 84 Norman Street and Muffie of 86 Norman Street. Following a brief discussion, no charges were preferred, as it was ascertained that both parties' vaccinations were up to date."*

It's a kind of code. The writer understands it; the experienced reader understands it; and our lawyers understand it. Here's another one:

"During the lively discussion on the extension of the Town water line to the Scotch Settlement Road, Councillor Ramsay was quite clearly overwrought. Mr. Ramsay is usually overwrought at evening council meetings and is sometimes overwrought as early as ten o'clock in the morning."

Because of all the long-standing feuds that simmer along the back roads of this community, you always have to remember that you're walking on eggshells. You just never know when what you write will make, as Shakespeare would have it, "ancient grudge break to new mutiny."

If you grow up here, the fractious nature of the community is just part of the furniture, and you don't even think about it much. But to a newcomer like Walt, it can be disturbing. Not that Walt has been sensitive to slander lately. On the contrary, nothing seems to bother him. He's been walking around with a perpetual grin plastered on his face ever since Maggie announced she was expecting.

September 25

Dear Ed,

I left Maggie sleeping this morning and stepped out onto the verandah. The first hard frost had come during the night, turning the cedar shingles and rail fences white. Wherever the first rays of sunshine landed, steam rose into the air.

I've seen this all before—and if you've had a child I guess you know this feeling—but it's as if I'm seeing it for the first time. And it's so beautiful. I just can't wait for our kid to see it all.

Not that we're taking anything for granted. Maggie's strong and healthy, but she's thirty-eight years old, having her first pregnancy. She had the amnio at week fourteen, and that was fine, but past the thirty-fifth week we have to have regular fetal assessments.

I don't know when Maggie will find the time. She hasn't slowed down on her chores, but it isn't that. It's the circle of women—cousins, aunts, neighbours, friends—who treat a pregnancy as a community project. The baby's room is full of socks and booties, blankets, quilts...soon there won't be any room for the baby. It's nice, but it's overwhelming.

And they're very prickly about protocol. There was so much competition over who would host the baby shower that Maggie had to arrange a series of smaller events to unruffle all the feathers. Freddy came over yesterday afternoon while Maggie was preparing for yet another prenatal get-together, baking enough chocolate eclairs to feed Napoleon's army. I was standing at the kitchen counter, grating lemons for a half-acre of lemon tarts. Even Freddy had been drafted and was grudgingly poking a single blueberry into each tart for decoration.

Maggie patted me on the shoulder as she went by. "They're just excited for us, Walt. They want to help."

"I understand that," I said. "But there's so many of them. You know, 'how many supervisors does it take...?'"

"You can't fight The Sisterhood," said Freddy. "I've seen 'em in action. They bring in the next-youngest kid and look at the twist of its hair—that tells 'em whether the baby's gonna be a boy or a girl. They float a needle on a thread over the stomach of the pregnant woman and watch which way it turns. And that's just the stuff they let us guys know about. I'm tellin' ya—don't leave your pets out after dark."

Maggie laughed. "Oh, stop it, Freddy. You'll frighten Walt. He's used to quiet, harmless women... on the floor of the stock exchange. And besides, a lot of the sisterhood are very experienced. They say they can tell that the baby's head size and shape are good, its pulse response to movement is normal, and it makes the right number of kicks per hour."

"You know I don't believe in mumbo-jumbo, Walt," she said seriously. "I do believe in the ultrasound. When you were in the city yesterday, Dr. Brigham did an ultrasound and it said the same thing. I think one should always get a second opinion."

She stepped out on the verandah to snip Johnny-jump-ups for the tarts, and Freddy leaned over to me.

"You got pregnant at the wrong time, Walt. The crops are off, the pickles and preserves are down, and these women have got time on their hands. I saw a coupla them down at Dry Cry's the other day, pickin' out the baby's first firearm."

In all fairness, it isn't just the women around here who regard a pregnancy as a public affair. I had the 4×4 at Ron's garage in Larkspur for the water pump at eight in the morning one day last summer and heard the following conversation over the snarl of impact air drills and the blare of Rock 95 radio:

"I think Helen's water broke last night."

"Yeah, I called Eric late and there was no answer."

"His car wasn't at the house this morning."

"I just did a lap of the hospital and it wasn't in the parking lot..."

"They'll have taken her to the Hillhurst Regional...she must have gone toxic like her sister."

And these were two bachelor mechanics in their early twenties. They'd correctly guessed that Helen Simpson was indeed in labour and had gone to the hospital, but because of an elevation in her blood pressure had been taken to the Hillhurst Regional, south of Highway 13.

Speaking of the water pump, it's had surgery four times now, and it's leaking again. I've watched Ron patch it enough times that I've sort of got the hang of it. Just takes a roll of Teflon tape and three hands. But this morning I decided I'd better get it fixed. Maggie's not due for a couple of months, but what if the baby's a "preemie"? I can't drive her to the hospital with the horses.

I was upside down in the engine compartment with a flashlight in my teeth, just getting the Teflon to a point where I could tighten it and make a seal...when it broke. Then the phone rang. I slithered back out and trotted over to the workbench for my remote phone. It was Freddy.

"How are you now, Walt?"

"Oh, I dunno," I said. "This damn water thing broke and I don't know what to do."

Freddy paused for a moment. "Are you gonna take her in, Walt?" he asked.

"I'm afraid to take her in," I said. "What if she seizes up on the highway?"

"You gotta take her in, Walt. Hang on, I'll be right over."

He hung up. I've never got used to the way people up here never say goodbye on the telephone. They just hang up. I went back to the 4×4 and stuck my head back down beside the radiator. The phone rang again. I squirmed out again and went back to the workbench. It was the Squire.

"I just talked to Freddy," he said. "He sounded kinda worried. He says this is it."

"It?" I snorted. "Well, maybe it is. She's been nothing but trouble since I got her."

"Walt," he said quickly. "Don't do anything, I'll be right over."

It's funny how they all get interested in a mechanical project at about the same time I'm ready to give up. The power windows don't work, the air conditioning quit last summer, the door hinges barely hold the doors in place. It just goes on and on. I took the phone with me on the next trip into the engine compartment. Sure enough, it rang again. This time it was Don.

"Walt?" he said. "I just talked to the Squire. He says you're talkin' kind of wild. Now, Walt, a lot of guys go through this; you're not thinking straight. You gotta take your time."

"Time?!" I scoffed. "Do you have any idea how much time I've wasted on this already? And there's no point being sentimental. I think I'm ready to drive her off a cliff somewhere."

The line went dead. A few minutes later, Don, the Squire, Freddy and the police officer from Larkspur arrived about the same time. Maggie appeared at the kitchen door with a tray of lemon tarts and leaned on the door frame.

"Well, I see nothing's changed around here," she sighed. "It still takes four supervisors for one man to work on a water pump. If we had a light bulb to change, we could get the whole Seventh Line down here."

Yours sincerely,
Walt

October 10

Dear Ed,

The Squire's real name is actually Baxter Fortescue, but nobody calls him that. I only know this because it's the name printed on the side of his mailbox. The Squire doesn't get a lot of mail. He does get a pension cheque once a month, but weeks go by without that little red flag going up. The only reason he goes out to the mailbox is to pull bird's nests out of it. I've watched him in a constant struggle with the blackbirds since I moved up here. This year he installed a 'bang' stick on the mailbox. It's a contraption they use for scaring birds out of orchards. It's basically an over-sized air gun that goes off every fifteen minutes or so. The blackbirds soon got used to it... but it gets the postman every time.

There's an unopened letter on the shelf behind the Squire's wood stove that appears to be about fifty years old. That could explain why he doesn't get a lot of return mail. It's propped up between a share stock certificate from the long-defunct Persephone Oil Shale Company and a Hillhurst County quarantine notice for rabies, dated 1923. When I dropped in on the Squire yesterday for a cup of coffee, I pushed a copy of the newspaper across the table to him. He squinted at the page through his reading glasses.

"What am I supposed to be looking at here, Walt?" he asked.

"Oh, it's the Auction Register," I said, pointing to the classified section. "There's a listing here on the Prince of Wales Road for an Augustus Fortescue. I was just wondering if that could be a relation of yours."

The Squire studied the listing for a moment and gave one of his short nods. "You could say that. He's my brother." He handed the paper back to me.

"Your brother? I didn't know you had a brother."

The Squire leaned back and turned to the window. "Sure is dry for this time of year," he said. "You know that damp spot up at the north end of the pasture? That used to be a pond. I got a bullfrog up there... he's three years old and he's never learned how to swim. What do you make of that?"

It was difficult to know what to make of it, all right. You know, Ed, I used to think that everybody up here got along like one big happy family. I'm finally beginning to realize that every second house along the concession road is nursing an ancient feud that dates back to the Crusades. The Squire has a brother he doesn't want to talk about, but it isn't just that. Freddy and the Squire have an ongoing fight about a steer. Calvin Currie and Don haven't really spoken to each other for four years since a famous incident when Don built his new state-of-the-art dairy barn and invited all the farmers in the area to an open house. I was standing next to Don when Calvin walked into the barn and stopped to gaze up at the spiderweb of steel truss work that supported the high ceilings. Calvin's a big man, a little past retirement age, and he has what I call the old dairyman's flinch. Forty years of bending over at the waist in a damp barn has given him a back problem that makes him wince every time he has to look up in the air.

"So, Calvin, what do you think?" asked Don.

Calvin made a noise in his throat like he was choking up a bug.

"Think?" he snorted. "Think what God could do if he had the money!" And he walked stiffly over to the lunch table to pick out a sandwich. Don was still sore about it an hour later when the last of the guests were departing. He watched Calvin climb into his weather-beaten pickup and jerk the door shut.

"That old skinflint," he muttered. "He's so cheap—you know he gave up drinkin' tea because he lost his tea bag."

I suppose we should be grateful that they don't take up blunt instruments and kill each other. They think it's more sporting to wear an opponent down slowly over a half-century. We went to a funeral last summer for an old guy who lived up in Pluto Township all his life. He and his wife looked like a normal couple. You'd see them together at the occasional Pancake Supper. I thought they were a little odd because she always rode in the back seat of the car. Well, it turns out they hadn't exchanged a single word in thirty-eight years. They actually divided the house into two parts. She lived on one side and he lived on the other. She still cooked his meals, but they never spoke. There was a little sliding door in the wall between the kitchen and his room, and she would pass a plate of food through to him and shut the door. Thirty-eight years!

Back at the farm, I told Maggie about the Squire's brother. She was sitting at the kitchen table, making some duck stencils for the baby's bedroom wall.

I said, "I can't believe I've known the Squire for five years and I didn't know he had a brother. I thought we were close."

Maggie nodded and smiled. "Don't feel bad. I've been around farmers all my life and I've never heard men talk about personal things much. I've always thought the rule is, you can talk about anything except what is on your mind. All I know is, the Squire and his brother haven't spoken since before I was born. The Squire was the younger brother, but he got the farm. That's pretty unusual, so maybe that's what started it. That's how most family disagreements get going. Between neighbours it only takes a poor fence or a dog killing chickens. For people farther away than next door, well it could be almost anything."

"Did your family feud with anyone?"

Maggie rolled her eyes. "Oh, sure," she said. "Mother put candles on the altar at St. Luke's in 1965 and the Lynches wrote a letter to the bishop. Called Mother a Papist. That one's gone on for two generations."

"Mrs. Lynch? The lady beside the Orange Hall? I thought you liked her!"

Maggie looked at me in astonishment. "Walt, how could you like a woman who uses Dream Whip to make a cream puff?"

I didn't have an answer for that one.

Footsteps thumped on the verandah and Don and Freddy appeared at the screen door.

"Come on in, boys," said Maggie. "Coffee's on and I just made scones. Ask them about the Squire's brother, Walt. They probably know more than I do."

"What, Lucky Gus?" asked Don. "What do you want to know?"

"Well, for starters, why is he called Lucky?"

"Luckiest guy living," said Freddy, as he slathered jam on a biscuit. "If that man shot at a pigeon and missed, he'd hit a moose."

"But he hasn't always been so lucky. I understand he lost the family farm to his younger brother."

"He did better than that!" exclaimed Freddy. "He got himself totally disinherited. The Squire was the one got chained to that hundred acres of sand hills and grey stone, and Gus was free to go off and make his fortune."

"Why was he disinherited?" I asked.

Don held out his cup for more coffee. "Gus ran off with a Catholic girl when he came back from the war," he explained. "It was a big scandal. The family was pretty staunch Orange Lodge. They cut him out of the will and wouldn't hear his name spoken in the house. What was her name?"

"Maureen Hoolihan," said Freddy with a knowing look. "And with a name like that, I wonder which foot she scratched with! Hmm?"

"Oh, yes. I remember," said Maggie. "Mum used to talk about her. They called her the Wildcat of the Pluto Marsh. She came out of one of those little shacks on the flats. They're all Catholics up there. She was like a wild animal. Red-haired, green eyes and ran around the country barefoot. My uncles were all warned."

"Ahh ... did she have horns and a tail?" I wondered.

Maggie looked at me frankly. "Whatever she had, all the boys wanted it. But I don't know, it all happened before any of us was born."

"All right," I said. "I'm putting this together. So, Gus ran away and was disinherited. What happened after that?"

"He used his veteran's money to buy a really good farm down near the city and he never looked back," said Don.

"A good farmer, was he?"

"Nope," said Freddy, reaching for the basket of scones again. "Terrible farmer. But the barn on that farm turned out to be just the spot where they wanted to build the clubhouse for the Woodbine racetrack."

"Aha," I said. "Lucky Gus."

"Lucky ain't the word for it," said Don. "I'd say he was carrying a tuba the day it rained gold."

"But this sale next month is not that far away," I pointed out. "It's just south of Highway 13. Which farm is that?"

"With all the money he got from the Woodbine farm, Gus bought three farms south of Highway 13. Now, the average guy only needs one farm to go broke. But Gus kept standing in the way of progress. One went for a gravel pit in the seventies and another went for a subdivision in the eighties. Now the last one's goin' for the Regional Hospital expansion. That's where the auction is. When that farm's gone, Gus'll have nothing left but the house and maybe twelve million dollars, poor fella."

"More good luck," I marvelled.

"Good luck?" snorted Freddy. "They used to say when Gus was down at Woodbine they never ran short of horseshoes. They'd just get him to bend over and they'd pull one out of his—"

Maggie raised one her stencil knives in the air as a warning. "Freddy! You're not at home with the boys. And there'll soon be a child in this house."

Yours sincerely,
Walt

October 15

Dear Ed,

It is an old custom in Persephone Township that, when a girl is married, they send her off to her new farm with a dowry of linens and cookware and livestock. I was the beneficiary of this wonderful tradition. Maggie came with a complete set of Blue Willow china, a spool bed that all of her ancestors have died in since 1870, six more sheep . . . and, of course, her nephews, Willy and Dave. Unfortunately, the old custom carries a strict rule about exchanges or refunds.

In some ways, Willy and Dave are as alike as two peas in a pod: they both have a high energy level and low risk perception. The only real difference between them is that animals love Dave and they hate Willy. Dave can load a herd of wild mustangs onto a trailer in the middle of a pasture armed with nothing but a carrot. Willy can't pull two rabbits out of a crate without causing property damage and personal injury.

Willy's been bitten by every dog in the township, including Luke, his own blue heeler. Usually, these incidents boil down to a simple case of ambush and counterstrike, but every so often he gets into a costly land war that drags out over a season.

One of these battles started last spring, when Willy picked up an old furnace oil tank from Isobel Meadows' place. Isobel has an almost-purebred dog we call a "borderline collie," named Pookie, who is really good with kids and has never bitten anybody. He does make a funny noise when he's excited. It's a rattling sound like a small electric motor starting up. Willy described the incident for us one day in the Red Hen.

"I was just tippin' the tank up into the back of the truck when I heard that noise...f-f-f-d-d-d-d-r-r...and felt hot teeth sinkin' into the back of my leg. I said, 'Oh, my goodness!'...and a couple of other things...and when I turned around I seen Pookie sneakin' under the hay wagon."

Isobel came out a few moments later and found Willy crouching under the hay wagon, taking wide, hard swings at the dog with a tire iron.

"Willy, what're you doing?" asked Isobel.

"I'm pickin' up that tank, Isobel. But first I'm gonna kill yer dog. He bit me."

"Pookie doesn't bite," protested Isobel.

"Oh, Pookie bites just fine," said Willy, rubbing his leg.

But the distraction was enough opportunity for Pookie. He disappeared behind the drive shed and Willy had to leave without squaring accounts. That was Round One. Round Two happened about a week later, when Willy was coming up the Seventh Line after breakfast at the Red Hen. Now, Pookie is not ordinarily a car chaser, but this day he hid behind the lilac bush by Isobel's mailbox and leapt out at the truck, causing Willy to jerk the steering wheel violently to the left, emptying a cup of boiling-hot coffee into his lap.

"My mind started workin' really fast," recalled Willy. "I figured once the burns started to blister I probably wouldn't be able to run, so I kicked open the truck door and headed down into the ditch after Pookie."

I know the place he's talking about. It's a very steep ditch. Not the sort of ditch you should take at a gallop in a blind rage and hot underwear.

"I actually got my hand on Pookie's tail, but Pookie turned left and I was pretty well committed to the direction

I was goin'—straight down through the crown vetch...you know that viney stuff with the purple flowers that the township sows along the roadsides to hold the banks. It grabs at your ankles like a bad dream, and before I knew it I was doin' a bobsled run without the bobsled. I was like the fella ridin' the tiger. I couldn't steer and I couldn't get off. I'd still be goin' today if it hadn't been for that barbed wire fence."

Isobel saw the truck sitting out in front of her house and went to investigate. She had to cut Willy out of the tangle of fence with a pair of pliers and drive him to the hospital for a tetanus shot. Willy stayed home for a couple of days, sitting in pool of Rawleigh's Ointment.

The following Wednesday, Willy drove by Isobel's and swerved again, this time right instead of left. He snipped off Isobel's mailbox with the side mirror.

"I'm real sorry, Isobel," he said, when he explained the incident to Pookie's mistress. "I had to swerve on account of yer dog. Like, he was right under my wheels and I coulda had him...I MEAN, I MIGHTA HIT HIM...and that woulda been just terrible."

That episode cost Willy forty-nine dollars for a new mailbox and two hundred dollars for bodywork on the truck and a new side mirror. Pookie was well ahead on points going into Round Four.

Yours sincerely,
Walt

October 20

Dear Ed,

People up here have a long-standing tradition of using one tool to do several jobs, and the tradition extends to

people's names. For instance, our farm is called the Old
Fisher Place, but Fisher is the most common name in the
township and that narrows it down to about four thou-
sand acres. If you look in the phone book, you will find
seven listings for A. Fisher at RR1 Larkspur. You're just
expected to know by the numbers that they refer to Allan,
Amos, Andy and the Anguses, that is, Angus B., Black
Angus, Square-ass Angus and Tight-ass Angus. Andy
Fisher often complains that, by the time he gets his mail,
"It's all wore out."

My neighbour Don belongs to a veritable dynasty of
Dons...there was Red Donald, Tall Donald, Donald the
Bold, Mad Donald...going back seven generations. Don's
oldest boy goes by the name of Young Donny. When I came
here, he was a gawky kid of fourteen with high-water pants
and a lot of acne. Now he's nineteen and he's filled out well.
He's bigger than I am. In fact, I think he's bigger than Don.
But he still calls me Mr. Wingfield...or sir...or both.

Recently, he's been dressing more carefully and has
become somewhat bookish. Maggie tells me this has to do
with the arrival of a new library assistant in Larkspur, a
girl of his age named Kim Dodd. She has long black hair
and a beautiful smile and goes about with a bare midriff
that has given a real boost to business for Carl's Custom
Collision out on the highway.

Donny can do anything with a car engine. He resur-
rected a '55 Chev pickup single-handed. He was helping me
locate a short in the ignition system on the 4×4 a couple of
weeks ago. He paused with the coil wire and the tester in
mid-air and frowned as if some profound insight into alter-
nating current had just occurred to him.

"Mr. Wingfield, sir," he said hesitantly. "You're pretty old, aren't you? I mean you're my dad's age..."

"I guess so," I said.

"But you married Mrs. Wingfield just about a year and a half ago. How'd you do it, sir?"

"What do you mean?"

Donny screwed up his face and shut his eyes for a moment. Finally he blurted out. "I mean...how'd you get her to marry you?"

I finished scrubbing the battery cable clamp I was working on. "Is this about Kim at the library, Donny?"

He grinned sheepishly. "Yes, sir, Mr. Wingfield." I smiled and turned back to the battery cable.

"So, you're having trouble telling her how you feel? Well, we all have trouble finding the right words at times. But when it comes right down to it, there are really only three words that a woman wants to hear..."

"Cables are backwards," offered Donny.

"No, not those words," I said, and the clamp went Kapow! in my hand. I stepped back and Donny relieved me of the cables and took over. I decided to focus on the answer to his question and let him handle the electrical work.

"Women love a grand gesture," I explained. "Something that says you're not afraid to tell the world how you feel."

Donny thought about this for a few minutes. Then he straightened up and grinned at me. "A grand gesture. Yeah...thanks, Mr. Wingfield..." It appeared that he had finally made up his mind about something, and I was humbled to be a part of such an important moment in his life. Just how important I was still to find out.

There's a new herbicide on the market this year called Grim Reaper. Farmers love it because, as they say, "It just kills everything!" Shortly after our conversation, Donny filled his father's field sprayer with Grim Reaper, went out to Don's high field on the town line, overlooking Larkspur, and wrote the words "I love you Kim Dodd" in acre-sized letters in a freshly planted crop of winter wheat. It was about a week before the herbicide took effect, making the letters turn stark brown against the beautiful green background. Maggie and I first noticed them when we were driving by on the highway and the sun came out on the hillside. The next thing I knew, Don was standing in my kitchen without a flicker of humour on his face.

"The boy says it was your idea, Walt."

"My idea ..." I stammered. "I was just ..."

"I figure every letter'll cost me a ton of winter wheat. I suppose I should be glad he wasn't sweet on that other girl at the library ... Henrietta Przbylowski. Do me a favour, Walt. Next time he asks you for advice, just keep it to yourself!"

He turned on his heel and left without another word.

Yours sincerely,
Walt

October 30
Dear Ed,

The feuds and internecine strife around here are starting to really worry me. And they're striking closer to home. I thought I knew the Squire, but clearly I don't. I made one innocent remark, and now Don isn't speaking to me. And then we heard that the new couple from the city, Professor Burns and his wife, got a real jolt. You remember he wrote that letter you printed objecting to a new factory hog barn planned for the township on the basis that it was inhumane for the pigs. Yesterday, he went down to get the mail and found a pig's head in the mailbox. It's just unbelievable.

If you're bringing life into the world, it should be into a garden. I'm not naive when it comes to this community. I didn't expect to find the Garden of Eden up here, but I did think I had found a place where neighbourhood meant something, a society of, if not love, at least tolerance and trust. Now I'm finding it's overgrown with discord and hatred. Is this a place to bring up a child? You might as well go back to the city, where anonymity gives the illusion of tolerance... where you can pretend to live peacefully with your neighbour because you don't know enough about him to think the worst of him.

Perhaps I'm being a bit shrill. The fact is, any garden needs work. Some of these old feuds will just have to be weeded out. It doesn't need a miracle worker. It just needs someone who will take the time and who knows what to do.

I have a book on my shelf that I found very useful at the firm, when I was responsible for a large staff of people. It's called *Making Peace in Your Workplace*. It's just chock full of good ideas. I've been flipping through it recently and I found a really good example. It's called the Borlov Technique. It goes like this:

> *Here the mediator's task is to find some object that has warm associations for both parties and use it as a focus for conversation...*

It's so simple, and yet so effective. Dr. Borlov was the famous United Nations mediator who had a brilliant career...until angry natives in Djakarta speared him to death in 1965. But there's a lot of really good stuff in this book. I read some of it to Maggie one night in bed, when she was having trouble drifting off.

"Walt," she said. "If you want to do something, why don't you see if you can get the Squire to go with you to that auction?"

It was a good suggestion. The day of Gus Fortescue's sale, I dropped in on the Squire. He was propped up on the sofa, reading *The Blazing Guns of Lost River Mesa*.

"How are you now, Walt?" he asked cheerfully.

"I'm fine, thanks," I said, taking a chair and plopping the picnic basket on the table. "Look, I thought I'd drive down to your brother's sale today. It's a beautiful day, Maggie's packed a lunch for us...ham and egg sandwiches, pumpkin pie, a couple of Newcastle Browns... Why don't you come with me?"

He sat up and rubbed his chin. Then he shook his head. "That's kind of you, Walt. But I don't think I will. Thanks for asking..." He glanced at the picnic basket. "Can I keep the lunch?"

"Sure," I said. It was none of my business, but I pressed on a little further. "You know, the notice says that they're having the sale because of ill health."

"Mm-hmm," he nodded. "I saw that. I wondered which one of them it was. I always figured Gus was too lucky to get sick."

"You don't know?"

"I know as much about them as you do, Walt. The last

communication I had was that letter from the Catholic woman he married."

I stood up and walked over to the wood stove and looked at the envelope. "So that's what that is. But you never opened it."

"Nope. You might let me know whether it's Gus or her that's poorly. The only time I ever hear anything is if someone tells me."

About fifteen miles south of Highway 13 I turned in the drive of Gus's farm. You can always tell farms that are getting a transfusion from some outside source. A half-acre front lawn with a sprinkler system, asphalt on the driveway, raised flower beds, a flagpole . . . Gus's farm looked like the cover for the Thanksgiving issue of *Country Guide Magazine*. I joined the registration lineup, which was set up in a renovated summer kitchen that served as a second entrance to the house. A middle-aged woman with unusually blue hair and a smoky voice wrote me down in her book and handed me a card with my auction number on it.

"All the way down from Larkspur, Mr. Wingfield," she observed.

"Yes, I believe Mr. Fortescue came from Larkspur originally. Is he here today?"

"Gus is here, all right," she replied. "But he doesn't get out of the house now at all." Her voice dropped confidentially. "He has the cancer, you know. That's why they're having the sale. Actually, his wife is right there. Maureen?" she called. "Mr. Wingfield here is from Larkspur."

A tall, graceful woman with white hair came across the room and extended her hand.

"Mr. Wingfield. How do you do?"

I shook hands with her and explained that I lived across the road from Mr. Fortescue's brother. She smiled.

"Baxter. Yes, of course. Please come in and meet my husband."

I followed her in through the summer kitchen down a large hallway to the front room. There, sitting in a soft chair by the window, was a tiny man wrapped in a quilt. He had a shock of white hair and an oxygen tube attached to his nose. He was watching the crowd on the lawn through the window. Behind him on the mantelpiece stood a number of framed black-and-white photos of a slim young man in the uniform of the Simcoe and Grey Foresters Regiment from World War II. Mrs. Fortescue touched her husband on the shoulder and he turned to look at me. He had the Squire's bushy eyebrows and high cheekbones, made even more prominent by the sickness.

"Augustus," she said. "This is a gentleman from home. Mr. Wingfield has the farm across the road from Baxter."

The old man made an effort at a smile. "How are things on the Seventh Line?" he asked in a hoarse whisper.

"Very well," I replied. "A bit dry, like everywhere else."

"You must be on the old Fisher place. Next door to the Haddocks."

"Mr. Wingfield is married to Mary Haddock's daughter Maggie," said Mrs. Fortescue.

"Yes, I am," I said in surprise. "How did you know that?"

Gus answered for her. "Maureen knows all about the families up there. She studies up on them like they was related to her."

"I was very fond of the old farm," she said. "Are any of the elms still standing? The ones in the laneway?"

"The Dutch elm disease got all but one, I'm afraid. I guess it must be the last one on the Seventh Line."

"I remember the elms," sighed Maureen. "Such graceful trees. The Baltimore orioles came to them every year and built nests and sang like opera singers. So noisy and full of life. I was so fond of the elms."

"The Sq...ah, Baxter," I corrected myself, "he wraps the trunk of that elm every year with sticky tape. It seems to stop the beetles. He's kept it going for years. I'll tell him you were asking after it, Mrs. Fortescue."

"Please call me Maureen," she said.

Gus coughed. "Lot of fuss over a tree. There's elms all over the place here. You never cared a fig for them."

"Drink your juice, dear," she said, placing the paper cup with a straw beside his pale hand. "You have to keep your fluids up." She turned to me. "We'll let him rest."

Outside, Maureen and I stood together under a large black walnut tree and listened to the patter of the auctioneer. I was surprised she had taken so much time with me on what must have been a stressful day for both of them.

"You know Baxter well, do you?" she asked.

"I thought I did. But I'm embarrassed to say I didn't know he had a brother until I saw the notice in the paper about the sale."

"That would be like him. They don't have any contact with each other, you know."

"Yes," I said. "That's one of the reasons I wanted to come today. It seems a shame, considering your husband's illness..."

"Yes, it is. How is Baxter doing, then?"

"He's fine. His memory comes and goes a bit, but basically he's fine."

"That's good. Please say hello to him for me... Goodness me...Look at that."

The auctioneer was taking bids for a white wooden porch swing with two rusty chains draped across it.

"That came from the home farm back in Larkspur," she explained. "It hung on the verandah. We used to rock in it for hours and hours. Oh, my. It's been lugged around from place to place all these years, but no one got around to putting it up. And there it goes. Excuse me, Mr. Wingfield, but I should get back to Gus."

She glided away across the yard to the house, nodding at people as she passed. She touched a woman on the arm and smiled; people made way for her. This was the Wildcat of the Marsh?

"Forty-two is bid," said the auctioneer. "Do I hear forty-five? Forty-five an-a-bid-a-bid-five-an-a-bid-a-bid-five-an-a-bid-a-bid-five?"

As he babbled away, I looked at the ancient porch swing and thought about its travels over the years. And then it occurred to me. Here was an object with warm associations for both parties. Dr. Borlov would certainly approve. I stuck up my hand and the auctioneer took the bid. After a brief canvass of the crowd, he knocked it down to me for forty-five dollars.

I drove back to Larkspur with the porch swing in the back of the 4×4. When I turned into the Squire's lane, I found him rolling up a hose on the front lawn. He straightened up and tossed the roll of hose beside the steps.

"I think the irrigation season is closed for the year, don't you?" he said. "Well, what do you know since we last spoke?"

"Gus is not well," I said. "He has cancer and I don't think he's going to last much longer."

The Squire took a breath and nodded. "That's too bad," he said. "I guess his luck's finally run out."

"I spoke to Mrs. Fortescue and she asked me to say hello to you."

The Squire looked at me sharply. "Oh, yeah? That's nice."

"And I have something for you from the sale. She thought it belonged back here at the farm."

I opened the back door of the 4×4 to show him the porch swing. The Squire blinked at it for a moment, looked at the ground and shook his head. When he looked up again, his face was hard and flushed. When he spoke, he used a tone I had never heard from him before.

"It's none of your damned business, Walter," he said, his voice thick with anger. "No business of yours at all. Now stop your meddling and leave me alone!"

He trudged away up the verandah steps and disappeared inside. The door banged shut behind him.

Yours sincerely,
Walt

December 5

Dear Ed,

At the beginning of December we got our first cold snap and the ground froze hard. But there still wasn't a puff of snow. Then the goat died. Mrs. Pankhurst was one of the oldest members of the staff. I brought her in during my second year to handle security for the sheep operation. She has presided over the farm ever since as an enforcer, dispensing justice with her hoofs and horns. I once asked Freddy how old she was.

"Geez, it's hard to tell with goats, Walt," he said. "But you see that one over there, the real bony one with the long beard that's havin' trouble walkin'? Well, this one of yours is the mother to that one over there."

Mrs. Pankhurst kept herself in fighting trim with regular workouts that included smashing her head against the barn door, which I eventually had to reinforce with quarter-inch steel plate. Visitors to the house would ask if I had a pile driver running in the barnyard, and I'd say, "No, that's just the goat."

Violence was in her nature, and it came as a surprise to me that she died of natural causes...sort of. She picked the lock on the stable door in the middle of the night and got into the feed room, where I store the sweet feed for the horses. At my age, I know better than to mess with mince pie after midnight, but Mrs. Pankhurst has been a risk-taker all of her life. She stuffed herself until her pancreas exploded and she died with a smile on her face.

This presented a problem. Because of the deep frost, burial on the property was out of the question, without some heavy machinery. Dead stock companies won't pick up sheep or goats anymore, and you can't take them to a landfill site. Most people around here just haul the carcass back to the bush for the coyotes, but it's an indictable offence under the Dead Animal Disposal Act.

I was reflecting on this when I got a call from Freddy.

"I'm just sitting here watching the soaps," he said. "Why don't we run her down to Scotty's mink farm in my truck? I need to get out for a drive anyway."

Maggie turned from the sink.

"Scotty's mink farm?" she protested.

"Well, I know it's not what we usually do," I replied.

"Chopped up and fed to the minks? It's not right to treat her like that."

"I know it isn't. But what am I supposed to do?"

Maggie has always felt that long-service employees should be laid to rest under the apple tree by the lane. If an animal dies in the middle of winter, she holds it in cold storage out in the pump house for spring interment.

"But she won't fit in the pump house."

"Go ahead, then," she conceded. "I guess there's nothing else for it. Oh, look. It's starting to rain. You be careful out there. It'll be slippery."

When Freddy arrived, we loaded the dear departed onto the bed of the pickup and Maggie placed a blanket over her. Freddy and I steamed off towards Larkspur. Out on the highway, Freddy glanced in the rear-view mirror.

"Uh-oh," he said. "Here's trouble."

I glanced back and saw a police car looming up out of the mist.

"He's not interested in us, Freddy. You weren't going that fast."

Freddy scowled. "They're always interested in a farm truck. This thing wouldn't run without all the Vise-Grips holding it together. The sticker's expired...I haven't got the new insurance certificate on me...and we're carrying dead stock without a licence, aren't we? This should be interesting."

I glanced in the side mirror. The cruiser lights were now flashing. Freddy steered carefully off to the side of the road with one hand while his other hand searched frantically under the seat for his safety belt. He found it and clicked it into the buckle. We both looked in the mirror and recognized the officer as Constable Bradley, a fairly recent addition to the Larkspur detachment.

"By gollies," said Freddy. "Look who we get today. Let the words of my mouth and the meditation of my heart be always acceptable in Thy sight." He rolled his eyes skyward and gave a quick sign of the cross.

Freddy speaks differently to this constable than to any other member of the force. I asked him about this once, and Freddy explained that the first time he was stopped by Constable Bradley his opening gambit had been: "Nice to see some sun for a change."

Constable Bradley replied, "The Lord makes his face to shine upon the unrighteous as well as the righteous." That day, the unrighteous received a seventy-five-dollar fine and lost three points for failing to yield.

Constable Bradley came to the driver's window. The rain was freezing to the brim of his hat.

"Good morning, sir. Do you have any idea how fast you were going?"

Freddy said, "I don't know, Officer. But it must have been fast. I had 'er right on the mat. We're on the Lord's business, Officer. We're taking a sick goat...to the vet."

Constable Bradley glanced in the back of the truck and saw the shape under the blanket. "Let's have a look here," he said, moving away from the window. Freddy scrambled out of the truck after him.

"Oh, Lord, be careful, Officer," he said anxiously. "We just got her quieted down. We don't want her to get violent again."

Bradley lifted the blanket and looked at Mrs. Pankhurst. "This goat is dead," he said.

"Oh, no!" gasped Freddy. "Gollies, I pray not, Officer. Grab that side mirror, Walt. Just give her a tug and she'll come off. Now hold her down, Officer." As the puzzled officer placed his hand on the goat, Freddy puffed quickly on the mirror and held it to Mrs. Pankhurst's nose and then showed it to him. "See, a little foggin'...she's breathin'," he assured the officer. "Real shallow, but she's still goin'...praise the Lord."

Bradley was nonplussed. "She's stiff as a board," he said.

"They go that way with the tetanus," said Freddy gravely. "But Dr. Jim has brought her back before, and God willing, he can do it again...if only we aren't too late..."

Bradley reflected for a moment, in a way that suggested he was not often given to such moments. "Do you want me to give you an escort into town?" he asked.

"That would be very good of you, Officer," said Freddy. "Time is precious to us."

The officer got back in his cruiser and skidded away with the lights still flashing. And Freddy gave hot pursuit in the direction of downtown Larkspur. I just looked at Freddy and shook my head, but he grinned at me like a pirate.

"Geez," he said. "This is gettin' more complicated than that soap opera I was watchin'. I hope it turns out better."

The wind was howling now. Branches lay across the road and a patch of black ice sent the truck into a short skid. "Careful, Freddy," I warned. "It looks pretty slippery."

We turned into the Larkspur Veterinary Clinic just as the good doctor was getting out of his car, coming back from lunch at the Red Hen. Seeing the flashing lights and sensing an emergency, he jogged over to the truck.

"Morning, Officer," said Dr. Jim. "What have we got here?"

Freddy stepped in quickly. "We thought it might be the tetanus again, Dr. Jim. Do you think you can save her?"

"Tetanus?" asked Dr. Jim with a frown. He looked at the officer and then at me and then he bent over to lift the blanket on Mrs. Pankhurst. Freddy and I held our breath. He straightened up and nodded his head.

"Yes...tetanus...I recognize the symptoms. Let's get her inside and we'll see what we can do."

As Freddy and I struggled with Mrs. Pankhurst, Bradley stood watching with a puzzled expression. "What causes tetanus, Doctor?" he asked.

"Oh, it can be a variety of things, Officer," replied Dr. Jim patiently. "Often it's contact with rusty metal. I had to attend to a cow this morning that had contact with a rusty farm truck out on the highway. In that case, tetanus was instantaneous..."

Freddy carried his end of the goat between the constable and the vet, gently nudging Dr. Jim towards the door of the clinic. "Ah...thanks fer all yer help, Constable," he said. "We sure wouldn't wanna interrupt you any further in the course of yer duties. God bless you for helping us out here this morning..." Bradley shrugged off Freddy's thanks and turned to go. Freddy hustled us towards the clinic, keeping one eye on the cruiser until it was safely out of sight. Then he dropped the goat. "Geez, that was a close one," he sighed. "I could just feel the dungeon door closin' on me this time. As the fella said, 'give me liberty or give me—'"

"Tetanus?" offered Dr. Jim testily. "I don't know what you two clowns are up to, but I've got some livestock to see to. There's a storm warning out. They've closed the highway north out of Larkspur. I want to finish up and get home while I can." He went back into the clinic, shaking his head in disbelief as he went.

"Well, looks like the road's closed to Scotty's," sighed Freddy. "We'll have to get a coffee and rethink our strategy. Let's throw her back on the truck, Walt."

All the usual suspects were gathered in the Red Hen, declaiming loudly about herbicides and pinto beans. Cigarette smoke and bacon fumes hung along the ceiling. Freddy and I had just got our coffee when the lights went out and the exhaust fans over the grill whirred to a stop. Donna, the waitress, moved to the blackboard above the cash register.

"Larkspur's power supply is gettin' more unreliable than Venezuela," she announced grimly. "We're on the blackout menu, boys. The special's changed from hot beef on toast with gravy to cold ham on bread with applesauce. You can have coffee...if you have it now."

The door opened and Don appeared, ice plastered down the front of his overalls. He didn't sit down, and the room went quiet.

"There's a bad storm coming in," he announced. "They say there's three separate fronts and they all got freezing rain. They figure it's gonna go on for a coupla days at least." He set his hat, turned and walked out again.

There was dead silence for a moment. Then a general scraping of chairs and zippering of coats as people rose and left. In a few minutes the café was empty, cold and dark. Outside the Red Hen, the falling sleet stung our faces as we looked at the sky. It had turned a weird purple colour. There was a distant rumble, like an approaching snowplow.

"By gollies," murmured Freddy. "That's thunder. You don't often hear that in the winter."

We looked in the truck bed. Mrs. Pankhurst was now encased in a clear coat of ice. She looked like the captain in the *Wreck of the Hesperus*.

> *Lashed to the helm all stiff and stark, with her face turned*
>   *to the skies,*
> *The lantern gleamed on gleaming snow and her fixed and*
>   *glassy eyes.*

"Well, geez, ain't it the truth?" agreed Freddy. "And then there's that other poet who said:

> *If we stand in the rain at ten below without a decent coat,*
> *It won't be long, I fear, before we look like this here goat.*

By the time Freddy and I got home, the roads were slick with ice and treacherous. Mrs. Pankhurst was frozen solid and welded to the truck bed, so Freddy just let me out at my gate and I walked down the lane to the house. Slid is more like it. The entire length of the lane was one vast sheet of ice.

For two months of the year, Persephone Township is like the south of France. The sun beats down upon the fragrant meadows, and gentle zephyrs waft through the trees. This is when most of the real estate is sold around here. For the other ten months, it's like...well...Persephone Township.

The winters are just ferocious. And the wind...I grabbed a tree at the halfway point to rest. We have our own species of conifer here, called the Persephone pine. They have branches only on the east side. I will admit that the township is not bad for bugs, though. I've only seen one mosquito on the farm in five years, and it had out-of-province plates.

I looked back out to the road, which was deserted. Ice-crusted twigs and branches dropped to the roadway from the maple trees in a steady clatter. Three days of this? It's impossible to move around; we'll be afraid to leave the house. Everywhere you turn in this township it's like being mugged. The people are hostile. Practically no one is speaking to me...Ed, I can get all this in the city!

When I finally gained the verandah and fell in through the kitchen door, Maggie was on the telephone. She said "Oh, my," several times and rang off.

"That was Elma," she said. "She says it's really bad south of us. Hydro poles are snapping like toothpicks under the weight of the ice. Her cousin Harry is a line-man, and he says we'll be without power for at least a week. Maybe more if the weather keeps up like this."

"A week!" I exclaimed. "What do we do? Are you going to be all right?"

"Oh, I'm fine," she assured me. "Nothing's happening. I think you'd better get togged up and go over to Don's. Young Donny's away this week and he'll have no one to help him in the barn."

As she spoke, a series of cracks like gunshots sounded outside the house, and we both turned to the window as the main branches of the maple on the front lawn crashed heavily to the ground. Ice chips smashed everywhere, making a sound like breaking glass.

I wrapped barbed wire over my boots and made my way gingerly down the road to Don's place, shielding my face from the wind and picking my way around fallen branches. I found Don chopping ice off the door of the root cellar, where he had stored his Y2K generator after the millennium scare wore off. I wasn't sure if he was still speaking to me, so I tried a fairly neutral opening.

"Is there ah...anything I can do?" I asked.

"Yeah," he nodded. "The fans are all shut down and ammonia builds up real fast in there."

"You mean the cows could suffocate?"

"Them and us both. We gotta work fast here."

State of the art is a terrific thing when you have electricity. When the fans are going, you'd never be aware that the slatted floors are located above a vast liquid manure tank. But when the fans shut down, a barn like Don's takes on all the ventilating properties of a quart sealer with a dead mouse in it. The smell of ammonia was thick enough to make my eyes water. We plugged the generator into the electrical panel, fired it up and watched as the fans slowly brought the barn back to life. After fifteen minutes, we could breathe again and I turned to go, when Don caught me by the elbow.

"As soon as we get the milking done, we've got to get the generator over to Bill Barnett's. I promised I'd be there by five o'clock."

We made it by six. Don put chains on all four tires of the tractor for the two-mile trip over to the Town Line. We didn't pass another vehicle on the way, which was fortunate because at times we were travelling sideways and needed both sides of the road.

Bill's cows were bawling because they were used to being milked by 4:30 p.m. By now, it was pitch dark. The three of us milked in the dim light of a storm lantern. We did all the feeding with a flashlight. Then Don and I hurried back with the generator to freshen up his cows again. At midnight we got a panic-stricken call from a farmer with a chick hatchery. His backup heat system had failed, and five thousand day-old chicks were in danger of freezing to death.

When we got there, Don had to take the panel apart and rewire it with a plug for the generator. We spent the rest of the night repairing the farmer's backup system. At daylight we staggered into Don's barn and found Don's wife, Elma, and the two younger kids sitting in the feed room in their coats.

"I figured they might be here," he said. "It's pretty murky, but at least it's warmer than the house. We have a fireplace, but it's electric."

"Look," I said. "We've got a wood stove..."

"No, I couldn't do that to you. Maggie's expecting the baby..."

I assured him she wouldn't mind one little bit. Elma and Don started the milking together, and I strapped on my barbed wire boots and made my way back to the farm, where I met Maggie on her knees on the verandah, piling wood into a wheelbarrow.

"There's no power anywhere within thirty miles," she sighed. "And there won't be for at least a week. All the roads are closed and they're calling for more freezing rain. The only buildings with a backup system are the school, the hospital and the arena, so they're setting them up as relief shelters. At least the phones work, so we can talk to each other."

I helped her to her feet and took over the wood job.

"I hope you don't mind," I said. "I invited Don's family here for the night. They don't have heat..."

Maggie nodded and patted me on the shoulder. "That's fine, dear. Four more doesn't matter at this point. That makes seventeen, now."

I went into the house and saw them all. Isobel Meadows was there with her new baby. She was very upset because she'd had to leave without her dog. Pookie had disappeared at the beginning of the storm and hadn't been seen since. There was Professor Burns and his wife. They'd built that odd-looking house up on the hill, the passive solar, geodesic, energy self-sufficient New Earth place. Apparently they bailed out after about three hours. Everybody was playing board games around the kitchen table.

I was surprised to see Mrs. Lynch coming out of the larder.

"You sure got a full house, Mr. Wingfield," she said cheerfully as she bustled by.

"Yes. Well, we're delighted to have you. We'll try to make you comfortable."

Mrs. Lynch put her hand on my arm and smiled. "Maggie, dear," she said. "I was just going to make up some cream puffs for you, but I see you're out of Dream Whip."

Maggie's eyes twitched, but she managed to return the smile. "You're right, I am. Maybe we'll just have to settle for some fresh cream."

When Don, Elma and the kids arrived, Don and I napped on couches for an hour before Willy and Dave burst in. Willy looked around at the clusters of people in various rooms.

"Hey, what have we got here?" he cackled. "The Christian Science Reading Room?"

I asked them what they had been doing.

"Errands of mercy, just like you," said Willy. "We've been chopping wood for the weekenders—"

"That's good of you," I said.

"—'cause they're the only people with wood stoves anymore. All the farmers are movin' in with them, and we gotta keep the precious farmers warm, don't we? Hey, cream puffs! Hi, Isobel, how're ya doin'?" Suddenly, he whirled and scanned the room. "Where's that dog?"

Isobel burst into tears.

"She had to rush here with the baby," said Maggie. "The Burnses have been down to look, but they couldn't find Pookie."

"That's too bad," said Dave. "It's not fit for man nor beast out there. I think we've got the wood problem covered for now, but there's beef cattle all over the place with no water for over a day now."

"There's lots of ice," I said. "Can't they just lick the ice?"

Don shook his head. "A cow needs twenty gallons of water a day. You can't get that licking ice."

So, while Willy and Dave went off to join the township crews clearing trees from the roadways, Don and I went off again with the generator, watering cattle and milking cows. This time, Professor Burns joined us. He pitched right in and helped carry pails, fork manure, wash cows' udders, you name it. We returned to the house for a supper of beef stew and bread baked in the wood stove. Then, too tired to sleep, the three of us went out to the haymow in the barn and sat in the open doorway above the barnyard, which gives a commanding view of the Seventh Line. We saw weird blue flashes of light on the horizon. We learned later it was from high-voltage transmission towers crashing to the ground. The only other lights to be seen were from snowmobiles buzzing here and there. It seemed odd that people still had the energy for snowmobiling after all the commotion.

Don explained to me. "That's the Kinsmen Snowbunnies out checking the houses. They're delivering candles and food to people and telling police about the ones who need to go to the shelters. It's dangerous work making a snow-mobile run on that ice." After riding the tractor around on it, I had to agree with him.

Two sets of flashing lights approached on the Seventh Line from the south. It was Dave on a four-wheel-drive monster tractor, the "small one" they use for blowing snow. Hooked behind Dave's machine was the Persephone Township Moose Bus, with its front wheels a few inches off the ground. This is the wretched old pink school bus they take to Kenora every fall for their annual hunting expedition. With the help of a tow truck lift, the boys had cobbled together an all-terrain personnel carrier. He turned into the lane, and we met Dave on the verandah.

"That's quite a people-mover you've rigged up there, Dave," said Don.

"Thanks! Say, have you seen Willy? He went off on his own a while back. Said he'd catch up with me."

Maggie pointed to the living room. "He just came in a minute ago, looking like Nanook of the North. He's getting warmed up by the fire."

We looked in and saw Willy bent over by the wood stove, whispering something to Isobel Meadows. He opened his coat sheepishly, revealing a shivering and bedraggled Pookie . . . with a strip of duct tape wrapped around his snout.

"F-f-f-d-d-d-r-r-r," growled Pookie.

"Ah, isn't that sweet," said Dave. "He's got Isobel's dog! Hey, everybody! Willy rescued Pookie!"

Willy glared at Dave. "Ahhh . . . shaddap!" was all he could say.

Yours sincerely,
Walt

December 10

Dear Ed,

On the morning of the third day, the sun rose in a clear sky and the temperature fell twenty degrees. For the first time I stopped to survey the devastation. My farm looked like it had been bombed from the air. Trees were down everywhere, and those still standing were stripped of their branches. Out in the orchard, all of the old apple trees lay crumpled under the weight of the ice. My new page-wire fence along the road had been crushed in a dozen places by fallen debris. Even the old mulberry tree had been pounded flat. It made me think of lines I'd memorized at school:

A little fire in human hearts
Will light the world and all its parts.
But fire blazing uncontrolled
Leaves the world in ashes, cold.
A little ice is like a balm,
It cools the world and makes it calm.
But ice on ice with no respite
Will crush the world and kill the light.

On the radio, we heard the mayor of the restructured community of Hillview announce a state of emergency. Now, when you do this in the United States, it triggers an immediate reaction. The government coffers for disaster relief open, the National Guard moves in, and the president flies over in a helicopter. It's not quite the same in Canada. Government offices are usually closed, journalists move in, and the prime minister flies south to the Caribbean.

In Ontario, our latest attempt to develop an emergency response procedure stalled in the definition stage. The committee just couldn't agree on what constituted an emergency. Finally, someone said, "Come on, people, let's start with the obvious—what's the worst thing that could happen here?" Hank Burford, the minister at the time, said, "An NDP victory."

Anyway, the mayor called the Department of Defence in Ottawa and was connected to a colonel who said the army could be sent, but the township would have to pay for it. Now, the complete property tax income for the township wouldn't cover the colonel's photocopying budget for the year, let alone the rental of the Queen's Own Rifles for a week. So the mayor hung up the phone and left the office, but, fortunately, he ran into a camera crew from *CBC Newsworld*. He explained the situation, and the army arrived about an hour after the next newscast.

When the soldiers got here, they were terrific. They fanned out across the neighbourhood, checking every house for signs of life. An armoured personnel carrier stopped outside Mrs. Coutts's house on the Town Line. The officer saw an oil lamp glowing on the kitchen table inside. He knocked; Mrs. Coutts came to the door and opened it a crack.

"Canadian Forces, ma'am," said the officer. "We're here to help."

"Oh, yes," said Mrs. Coutts.

"Do you need food, ma'am?"

"No."

"Do you need any water?"

"No."

The officer looked around and saw a pile of maple logs in front of the house.

"Well, there must be something we can do. Can we split that pile of firewood for you?"

Mrs. Coutts peered around him at the wood and thought about that for a minute.

"Yes," she said, finally. The men leapt into action, split three cords of wood and stacked it on her verandah. When they were done, Mrs. Coutts peeked out the door again and became downright chatty.

"Why, thank you, boys. That's very kind of you to do all that for me," she said. And she gave them a cup of tea.

"Just part of the job, ma'am," said the officer. "How long have you been without power?"

Mrs. Coutts thought about this for another minute.

"Seventy-two years," she said.

I was helping Don with the milking again this after-noon and suddenly found myself very short of breath. I asked Don if he would mind if I stepped outside for a minute. To my surprise, he came out with me and we both sat on the tailgate of the truck. It turned out he was having trouble breathing, too.

"The trouble is, that little generator will run the venti-lating fans, but it don't have enough juice to run the compressor, too," he complained. "So I have to turn the fans off to get enough pressure to run the milking machines. In twenty minutes, the place fills up with ammonia again and I have to throw the doors open. That's a great way to give the cows pneumonia, because they're used to a warm barn. So, either I'm suffocating or I'm standing in a cold wind. I don't know what to do."

I looked up to see Calvin Currie turning in the lane in his old Dodge pickup. He drove up to the barn beside us and switched off the engine.

"Hi, Calvin," I said.

"How're you now, Walt?" Calvin gave me a quick nod and eased himself stiffly out of the cab. He turned and fished around in the front seat for a moment, looking for something.

"I think you need a bigger generator, Don," I said. "I wonder if there's anyplace . . ."

"Can't be found," said Don. "I've called everywhere. And they say they've got to rebuild the power grid all the

way up from Highway 13. It could be weeks before we're
back up and goin'."

Calvin emerged from the truck cab and heaved the
door shut with a bang.

"You know, Don," he said. "A milker only needs ten
or twelve pounds of vacuum pressure, and years ago,
when the power went out, we used to get that from the
farm truck."

"How'd you do that?" asked Don.

"There's enough vacuum in the carburetor to run the
windshield wipers, right? So, if you run a small diameter
hose, about an inch maybe, from the air cleaner on the
truck to the milk line, you can get enough pressure to run
a milker, maybe even two with that souped up '55 Chevy
yer boy's got there. Then you can milk and run the fans at
the same time. You get me?"

"Don," I laughed. "You're going to have to ask Donny if
you can borrow the car tonight."

"One-inch hose..." said Don, carefully. The two men
eyed each other.

"Yeah," grunted Calvin. "I brought a roll of it with me.
And a coupla adapters..." He lifted the plastic shopping
bag he was carrying. "If it's any use to you. Maybe you got
the problem licked already. I was just goin' by and wondered if you'd thought of it."

"You were just goin' by, were you?" asked Don. Calvin
doesn't use the Seventh Line except during the summer,
when he's checking cattle on the pasture across the road
from me.

"Yeah, I got some fence down over here...I'll have to
do something about it in the spring."

In fifteen minutes, Calvin's vacuum system was installed and running two milkers. Don could now milk and breathe at the same time, and I could see that his working life might return to something approaching normal. Calvin grinned.

"What do you think of that?" he said, to no one in particular.

Don nodded. "Yeah. I guess it works... Thanks for the idea."

"You got a nice barn here," said Calvin, squinting at the truss system above him.

"Oh?" said Don skeptically. "I thought you didn't like it."

"What's not to like? Lovely place to work. I would have put one up myself if I could."

"Then why didn't you?"

Calvin sat down on the concrete manger. "I couldn't do it," he said. "But that don't mean I don't like your barn. It was different for us. When Mary got the Parkinson's, that left me on my own. I had to redo the house for her, pay for a nurse, wheelchair and stuff. I had to make that old barn pay every day, all year. I couldn't think twenty years out the way you did. It was just different, you know? No, this is the way to do her, if you can swing it." He sighed and nodded to himself, looking around at the barn.

We talked for a little while and Calvin eventually went on his way. Don didn't say anything for a long time. While we were washing the milking equipment in the sink in the milk house, he finally broke the silence.

"You know, that old guy's smarter than I give him credit. He's looked after a sick wife for ten years with twenty cows and a cream cheque. He doesn't owe a dime to anybody. And he could make a water pump out of juice cans and a coupla rubber bands. Maybe I'll get him back here and see if he can hook up the stereo system."

— • —

The thaw we were all praying for didn't happen. The fourth and fifth days we got wind and snow. The snow hid the black ice in spots, making the footing even more treacherous for man and snowplow. The roads drifted so badly we wondered if they'd ever get cleared. If we wanted to get into town, we had to organize a convoy for safety—if one car got stuck, then the others could shovel and tow it free.

But the thaw in the human condition was remarkable. Gradually, our seventeen house guests departed, having managed to arrange food and heat in their own houses. There was a lot of laughing and hugging and even some tears with the farewells. Young Donny was back in his father's good graces, not just because of the '55 Chevy. It seems some aerial footage on the national news picked up Donny's message in the winter wheat and the chamber of commerce for Larkspur wants to talk to Don about next year.

Don and Calvin Currie have become fast friends, a roving pit crew specializing in low-tech solutions to difficult problems. For example, the stoves and the furnace in the Orange Hall in Larkspur run on natural gas, which was still in service, but the system was useless because the gas valves are triggered by electricity. So is the fan motor on the furnace. Calvin guessed that a twelve-volt battery with a small transformer would run the relay switch on the gas valves. And Don rigged up a chain drive for the furnace fan using a stationary exercise bike. Young Charlie Teeter's training program for the provincial cycling championships was all shot by the storm, so they recruited him to provide the muscle power on the bike. Calvin joked that with Charlie pedalling they could pump enough hot air to run an election campaign.

News travelled fast. The masters of the Orange Lodge threw the doors open to the public as yet another relief shelter. They set out sleeping bags and cots and prepared to serve hot dogs and soup to all comers. Everybody came, but they weren't looking for food or shelter. They were looking for company. With no TV or video games at home, the kids rediscovered the old bowling alley in the basement. Mrs. Lynch started playing the hall piano.

When the ladies of the community were informed they could operate the hall gas stoves again, they announced an impromptu supper of the combined auxiliaries of the Anglican and United Churches...Freddy calls it the Ladies Artillery. Everyone dashed home to salvage food that had been left outside to freeze.

As the daylight faded, candles were lit and kerosene barn lanterns glowed from the ceiling. I sat beside Mrs. Lynch on the piano bench and listened to the place humming with the sound of human community...of something like harmony...except for the Squire, of course. I saw him a couple of times across the room, but he didn't look my way. I sat beside Mrs. Lynch on the piano bench as she paused between tunes. She looked around the hall and her face softened.

"You know, it was like this when I was a little girl, before the electrification," she said. "The winter was long and cold and dark, and it took nearly all of your energy to keep warm and fed. But then, it was the only time you really saw people. The farm work was all done and the roads were good, packed with snow. It was the visiting time. Oh, yes, it was just like this."

"Do you suppose the people in those days really got along any better than they do now?" I asked.

"They had their battles, that's true. I don't think that ever changes."

"I mean, here we are sitting in the Orange Lodge, an anti-Catholic organization dedicated to the nursing of ancient grudges. No wonder people don't get along. It's institutional."

"Oh, nobody pays any heed to that business anymore," she scoffed. "This year they cancelled the Orange Parade because one of the Orangemen was sick and the other one didn't want to march alone. Who cares if you're Protestant or Catholic these days?"

"Lots of people, apparently," I said, nodding towards the Squire.

"What?" she exclaimed. "Not the Squire. Oh, no, you're very wrong there, Walt. The Squire has no problems with Catholics. Why, he wanted to marry a Catholic girl."

"He did? Who was that?"

"Let me think. Her name was Maureen Hoolihan. Lovely girl. Such a shame. She ended up marrying his brother, and we don't see her anymore."

Just at that moment Freddy appeared at my shoulder and grabbed my elbow. "We got trouble here, Walt," he whispered. "Pookie broke the ceasefire. He took the seat out of Willy's pants this morning and got away clean. Willy's just come in and he's packin'."

We found Willy and Don in the coatroom at the hall entrance. Don was blocking Willy's passage into the hall, and Willy was fuming.

"It ain't right, Willy," Don was saying. "There's kids here."

"This town ain't big enough for the two of us," declared Willy. "I was carryin' a flat of eggs for Pete's sake ... for the nursing home. Then I hear that noise ... F-f-d-d-r-r-r-r. I just squirmed up like a spider on a hot stove lid. You could have plugged my ass end with a turnip seed, I tell you."

"What have you got there, Willy?" I asked.

Willy opened his jacket to reveal a short electric cattle prod in one pocket and a can of ether in the other. I just shook my head.

Willy was adamant. "I'm not gonna start anything ... but a man's got a right to defend his person."

"It'll probably be okay, Don," I said. "Pookie's tied up to Isobel's chair way up at the other end of the hall."

"All right, you can go in," said Don. "But stay down here, Willy. Let's keep a lid on this thing."

The buffet tables sagged under the weight of strip loin steaks, smoked salmon, seventeen salads, scalloped potatoes, coq au vin, breads, cheeses, fruit and an exotic array of desserts. The combination of candlepower and over a hundred warm bodies sent the temperature and humidity in the hall up sharply. Charlie Teeter had stopped pedalling and was loading up two plates with carbohydrates. Calvin and Don had rigged up a simple clockwork winding mechanism to run the ceiling fan over the buffet table. You pull a chain attached to a ratchet that tightens the spring beside the fan. It's ingenious, and the fan runs for about fifteen minutes. It was just whirring to a standstill when Willy, Don and I went through the buffet line together.

"Many's the poor family has to make do and call this a meal," laughed Willy, helping himself to a large portion of beef tenderloin. I was just pouring myself a glass of Chateau Margaux when I heard the minister from St. Luke's behind me.

"It sure is stuffy in here," he complained. "Oh, ye winds of God, bless ye the Lord!"

He reached up and pulled down on the chain of the ceiling fan. The ratchet turned, making a rattling sound like a small electric motor starting up. "F-f-f-d-d-d-r-r-r-r-r-r-r-r—"

What happened after that was something of a blur. Willy whirled and fired. A wild jab with the cattle prod sent the poor minister headfirst into a Savannah Cream Cake. A blast from the ether can passed over the chafing dish and sent a sheet of flame the length of the buffet table. Women screamed. The piano stopped. When the smoke cleared, Willy was lying in a pile of potato salad. The minister sat on the floor, dabbing at sticky red fluid drenching his shirtfront.

"My God, I've been shot!" he exclaimed.

Freddy knelt down beside him and handed him some napkins. "You're okay, Reverend," he said soothingly. "That's just raspberry purée. It comes out after a couple of washes."

Don frog-marched Willy to the coatroom and disarmed him. Freddy threw Willy a towel and trotted back out and up onto the stage to calm the crowd.

"Okay, folks," he said. "Okay. There's nothing more to see here. Go back to your suppers and we're gonna have us some entertainment. Mrs. Sniderman? Come on up here. Mrs. Sniderman's gonna sing 'Marble Halls' for us, folks. Mrs. Lynch, pound out a verse to get her going, will ya?"

Mrs. Sniderman is a big woman...as Freddy says, "Big enough to burn diesel." As a soprano, she has tremendous stamina. She sang "Marble Halls," "How Great Thou Art," "Softly and Tenderly Jesus Is Calling" and appeared to be just getting warmed up. Freddy leapt up on stage again.

"Thank you, Mrs. Sniderman," he said, clapping enthusiastically. "I'll bet they heard that down in Lavender. Now we'll get back to you, but the first thing you want in a variety night is some variety."

He pulled a crumpled sheet of paper from his back pocket and consulted it. "What have we got here? We got a great show for yas here tonight. The Marshall Sisters are the synchronized swimming champs for Hillhurst County...and they do some step-dancing, too." He grinned at the crowd. "I guess we'll go with the step-dancing, huh?

"Then George McCormick's gonna come up here and do his ear stand...and if you haven't seen this, you're in for a real treat. It looks pretty much the way it sounds. He'll need a door frame. Then either we could have seven-year-old Roberta Przbylowski to do her intermediate program on the trampoline...or I could play the accordion. You know the difference between the accordion and the trampoline, don't you folks...? You take off your shoes before you jump on a trampoline!

"While everyone gets ready, I shall recite a poem written especially for this occasion, entitled 'The Ballad of the Great Ice Storm.'"

Along the line of western hills the thunderclouds will form
Till even the guys at Environment can see she's coming on
    to storm,
But she'll have to pack a helluva whack and chill us to the
    bone
To come anywhere near the awful storm that iced up
    Persephone.

It struck on Thursday afternoon and swept across the
    region.
Honest folk fled to their homes; it even emptied out the
    Legion.
The ice built higher on every wire, falling branches found
    their mark,
And supper found us without heat and sittin' in the dark.

"Now isn't this an awful sight," I said, surveying that
    scene.
There ain't a tree left standing twixt here and Road 13.
You cannot walk a single block, the sidewalks are like
    glass,
And if you put a foot down wrong, you fall flat on your
    face.

Oh, what can you do when the rain comes down and
    freezes cold and white?
And the price of beer and candles has tripled overnight?

Well... you learn to curse in rhyming verse and plot some
   way to fly
And yank the motor outa' that great Zamboni in the sky.

I glanced over at Maggie and saw that she was holding her sides and rocking with laughter. She looked as though she would...and then I realized she was...

"Oh, Walt!" she gasped. "The baby! It's coming!"

Mrs. Lynch and I helped Maggie into the Regalia Room, where the banners and stuff are stored for the Orange Parade. A cellphone appeared out of nowhere and I tried to call the doctor. I couldn't remember the number.

Maggie took a breath and said very clearly: "Four, three, five, five, oh, five, eight." I pressed the numbers carefully and got that all right. The message said that the doctor was at the Regional Hospital south of Highway 13. More numbers and we finally connected.

"Doctor, the baby's coming and it's early!" Maggie says that I was shouting at this point.

"Early is a relative term, Walt," replied Dr. Brigham patiently. "The date I gave you was an educated guess. Maggie's in good health. We know this from the office visits. You just keep her warm and comfortable and we'll see how things develop."

"But we've got to get her to the hospital!"

"I'm afraid Larkspur Hospital is pretty much out of commission right now," said the doctor. "Most of the patients have been moved here to the Regional. I think you might be better to sit tight right where you are until I can get there."

"We're in the Orange Hall. Is that safe?"

"Safe is a relative term, Walt. You roll the dice every time a woman goes through childbirth, and ninety-five percent of the time it's completely routine. You just stand there and catch it. Now, if you're at the Orange Hall, you have a retired obstetrical nurse living right next door. Gertrude Lynch. Do you think someone could find her?"

"Mrs. Lynch? She's with Maggie right now."

"Excellent," said the doctor. "Good. I want you to tell Mrs. Lynch that I'll need pulse, blood pressure and temperature for the mother, dilation, fetal vitals...that sort of thing."

I put my hand over the phone and said, "Mrs. Lynch... the doctor needs Maggie's purse and her mother's thermal underwear and her fighter beetles..."

"For Pete's sake, gimme that," said Don. His big hand closed over the phone, and he handed it to Mrs. Lynch.

"Yes, Doctor," said Mrs. Lynch. "Her pulse is seventy-eight, temperature normal, cervix dilated five centimetres... yes, I'll just slip over and get my things now."

She passed the phone back to me and went briskly back to Maggie.

"Walt, it sounds like everything's progressing very well," continued the doctor. "I don't think I need to be there at all."

"But what if something goes wrong?" I protested.

"The army's right here, Walt. In the unlikely event there's a complication, I can be there in a helicopter in fifteen minutes."

In less than a minute, Mrs. Lynch bustled back into the room with a bag, checking a list she had made. "Yes, I've got everything here...except...oh...! I'll need a roasting pan . . . We've got one in the hall kitchen. Marjorie?"

"A roasting pan?" I said. "Doctor, please! You've got to get here somehow!"

"Walt," said the doctor soothingly. "Maggie's in good health and in good hands. Frankly, if it's a choice between a normal childbirth with Mrs. Lynch attending and me climbing into a Canadian army helicopter built in 1964, I like Maggie's chances a lot better than mine. Now, I have to slip away, Walt. Call me if there's any change." And he rang off.

Mrs. Lynch was sitting next to Maggie, listening to the baby's heartbeat with a fetoscope. Maggie was quite pale and her forehead was covered with sweat. But she was quiet for the moment.

"And how are you, dear?" said Mrs. Lynch. "Are the pains stronger now? How far apart are they?"

"About four minutes, I think," whispered Maggie. "I think they're coming again."

Mrs. Lynch took her by the shoulders and said, "Get a deep breath into you, dear, that's it."

Maggie breathed deeply and her eyes widened. "I think I'm gonna . . . throw aaaaaaagghh!"

Mrs. Lynch grabbed a wastebasket and plunked it in front of Maggie as she retched.

"There you go," she said. "You just honk into that, honey. That's your body's way of getting ready to do battle." She turned to me and spoke in crisp words that would have sent a platoon of men scampering out of a trench into gunfire. "You want to get her two wet towels, Mr. Wingfield . . . one hot and one cold."

"I can't sit down," moaned Maggie. "I can't sit."

"That's good," approved Mrs. Lynch, helping Maggie to her feet. "Walking's the best thing for you, if you can do it. C'mon, dear, take my arm and we'll look at these pictures on the wall. What do we have here? Oh, my goodness, there's the massacre of the Protestants at Castle Kerry. Not as restful as the new labour room at the hospital, is it?"

She was terrific. She took Maggie's vital signs and the baby's heart rate every half hour and checked the dilation of the cervix. She got Maggie to breathe through the contractions. I timed each one and counted out loud for her so that she knew when they were coming to an end, and when they finally stopped and she called for a cloth I mopped her brow, first with the cold cloth, then the hot cloth, sticking a Popsicle in her mouth and smearing her lips with lip balm.

So it went until one o'clock in the morning, the contractions getting closer and closer and more and more powerful, until finally Maggie dropped to her knees and crushed my hand in hers.

"I can't do this anymore!" she wailed.

"That's what we like to hear!" cheered Mrs. Lynch. She turned to me with a knowing smile. "They always say that when they're ready to pop." She helped Maggie back onto the cushions. "Yes, you're going to have a little baby now, Mrs. Wingfield. You've done a wonderful job, and it's just going to take two or three more pushes and we'll be all done. It's all right to push now. Are you ready...? Now... PUSH!"

Maggie pushed with all her might. The baby emerged on the third try.

"There she is!" cried Mrs. Lynch. "Look at her, the little purple bundle of grief that she is. You have a little girl. There's your Hope, Mrs. Wingfield. And she's just perfect, so she is."

Mrs. Lynch cut the cord, tied it off and gently laid the baby on Maggie's chest. After a minute, she wrapped her in a warm towel and placed her in the roasting pan. Then she handed her to me.

They tell me babies can't see anything at birth because their eyes don't focus. But I have strong doubts about this theory. The baby's eyes opened wide and stared straight at me, such a look of skeptical appraisal as I have ever received from anyone in my life.

I heard voices and then a cheer from the main hall. I opened the door a crack and saw a sea of faces. They were all still there. I stepped out with Hope in the roasting pan and held her up for everyone to see. There was another cheer.

"It's a g-g-girl," I stammered. "Her name is Hope."

Fortunately, they cheered again, because I couldn't say anything else.

Yours sincerely,
Walt

December 15

Dear Ed,

The next week was, let's say . . . busy. If you think a newborn is a handful at the best of times, try having one when the power's out, supplies are scarce and to get to the road you still have to crawl on your hands and knees up the lane. Never mind, it's been the best week of my life.

Everyone has helped. Mrs. Lynch has been over every day. She even brought her last can of Dream Whip to make cream puffs. Now, Maggie is a woman who will never eat crow—but she ate the Dream Whip.

Yesterday afternoon Hope was napping, Maggie was on the phone, and I was piling wood on the verandah, when I heard a crack like a cannon shot. The great elm tree in the Squire's lane crashed to the ground. As it went down, it took the power line, a fence and the Squire's pump house with it. Maggie came out on the verandah. She looked at the fallen elm tree, but she clearly had something else on her mind.

"That was Maureen," she said. "Gus is dying, and she can't get hold of the Squire because his phone is out. She says Gus wants to come home. The hospital's in chaos right now, and there's nothing more they can do for him there, anyway. He just keeps asking her to take him home to the Seventh Line."

I couldn't make any sense of this. There were so many questions. The Squire wanted to marry Maureen, but she went off with Gus. Why would Gus want to come home?

"I don't know," said Maggie. "But I think we've been wrong about all of this. She said something odd on the phone. She said she knew it might be hard for the Squire, but she feels she's been a disappointment to Gus in many ways and just this once she wants to 'do the right thing by him.' She said it twice."

I looked over at the Squire's house. With all of the trees now gone between us, it seemed a long way off. The porch swing I'd bought at the auction was sitting at my feet. I remembered how Maureen had said, "We used to rock in it for hours and hours."

The walk over to the Squire's was treacherous, but it wasn't the walk I was worried about. I picked my way up the lane and across the road, climbed over the fallen elm tree and up the walk to the Squire's front door. The Squire was waiting in the doorway.

"Hell of a mess out there, isn't it?" he said.

"I'm sorry about your poor old tree," I replied.

"Yeah. We won the battle and lost the war. At least those damned elm beetles didn't get it. It took the power line down with it too. Did you see that? I'm going to need an electrician; that is, if we ever get the power back. And look at all the—"

"Maggie just got a call from Maureen. Your brother is dying and he wants to be brought home here to the house."

"Home? After fifty-five years he calls this his home?"

"Maureen wants to know if you will allow it. I can't imagine it will be for very long. We'll have nursing care around the clock, and you know everybody is here to help. Maureen said she is anxious to spare your feelings, as well."

"What would she care about my feelings? She walked out of here all those years ago and never looked back."

"Are you sure about that?" I asked.

"Oh, she sent me a letter to explain it all." He tossed his head in the direction of the wood stove.

"But you never opened it . . . Don't you think you should open it now?"

The Squire was silent. Finally, he motioned me to come in. He stood looking at the envelope on the stove for a long time. Then he carefully picked it off the shelf and ran his thumbnail along the seal. He removed the letter gingerly, unfolded it and stared at it for a moment. Then he handed it to me and looked away.

"Would you read it?" he asked gruffly.

I took the letter. It was written on robin's egg blue paper in a poised, elegant hand and dated November 17, 1945. I read the words out loud to the Squire:

Dear Baxter,

I'm writing this late at night because I can't sleep and I want to say what is in my heart.

I have had many second thoughts since Gus asked me to marry him. He's a fine man, but I can't seem to forget the time you and I spent together, in spite of all the difficulties with your parents.

I know it's important for you to obey your parents' wishes, but I also know that I love you, and if you love me too, then I feel everything else will work itself out somehow.

If you say the word, I will tell Gus I'm sorry, that I can't marry him next Friday. It may be hard for him, but I know it will be for the best.

Hoping to hear from you.

All my love,
Maureen

I folded the letter and handed it back to him. "I'm so sorry," I said. He took it, raised it slowly to his face and sniffed the paper. Then he folded it back into the envelope and replaced it on the shelf of the wood stove. Finally, he spoke.

"You tell Maureen that Gus can come home."

Back at the house, Maggie and Hope were waiting at the kitchen door. I told her what had happened.

"It seems such a waste," I said. "Why on earth would he not have opened that letter?"

"There's a difference between not needing to know and needing not to know," said Maggie slowly. "My guess is he thought the letter said one of two things . . . and he couldn't really live with either."

Late the next afternoon, an ambulance appeared on the road from the south. Maggie and I bundled up the baby and made our way over to the Squire's. The elm tree blocked the lane, but they backed up the ambulance as far as they could. The back door opened and the stretcher emerged. I caught a brief glimpse of Gus's gaunt face, eyes wide open and fixed on the house. Then shoulders and hats obscured my view as they carried him forward.

He didn't make it. He died before they could get the stretcher over the fallen elm. Maureen knelt at his side for a few minutes, her hand on his. Then she made the sign of the cross and allowed herself to be helped to her feet. She looked around at the crowd of neighbours, smiled faintly and took a deep breath.

"There . . . it's done," she said. "He saw the house. Poor Gus. Thank you so much. Thank you all so much." She looked up to the verandah and saw the Squire. "Oh, Baxter. There you are. What a commotion we've made for you this afternoon. Here, Mr. Wingfield, take my hand. I can't stand on this treacherous ice."

I helped her over the last of the elm trees and up the steps to the Squire. He took her hand and they stood looking at each other for the first time in over fifty years.

"I just read your letter yesterday," said the Squire.

"Yesterday?" said Maureen.

They looked at each other for another long moment, and then the Squire held the door open for her and they went inside together. I made my way back up the lane to Maggie and Hope. We stood and watched as the ambulance slowly backed out of the laneway onto the Seventh Line, paused and headed back south.

"What do we do?" I asked her. "What will become of them?"

"Who knows, Walt? We'll just have to make sure she knows she's always welcome here."

"Yes, we can do that. What do you think, Hope?"

Hope made that gllliggggccchh sound that babies make so that we can fill in the words for them. Across the road, the small group of Gus's mourners lingered beside the fallen tree, the way people often do outside a small country church after a service. It was a scene in black and white that made me think again of fire and ice.

Sometimes it's hard to tell the difference between the two. For the Squire and Maureen, their fire acted like ice—it made their lives cold for half a century. For the folks around here, the ice acted like fire—it warmed them and brought them a bit closer. But it also had the same effect as a forest fire—it cleared the ground for a fresh start. A fresh start and a new Hope.

Yours sincerely,
Walt

Another note from the editor:

The Great Persephone Ice Storm cleared the ground, all right.

For one brief, shining moment, peace and harmony prevailed across the township. Which was great news for everyone, except the newspaper. I was dismayed to realize how much I rely on hatred and discord for my livelihood. When the lion lies down with the lamb, it means a sleepless night for the editor.

There were some lasting changes to the landscape. When they restored the power to the Town Line, the crews were in such a rush they accidentally put a pole in Mrs. Coutts's yard and hooked her up to the grid. When they realized their mistake, Mrs. Coutts told them not to worry—she was sure it would come in handy. That "terrible ice storm" had taken down the pole for her clothesline.

The mayor received a cheque for thirty thousand dollars from the Federal Disaster Relief Fund. The town fathers used the money to buy a Zamboni for the arena. Ernie Pickets has been doing the job for years in a pair of snow boots, hauling a perforated oil drum. He was thrilled he'd get to drive it, and he was the one who suggested entering it in the books under Ice Relief.

Professor Burns went down to his mailbox and found a smoked ham in it, with a note saying, "Thanks for the help. You're a good neighbour."

But in some ways, things are just the same. The day after the lights came back on, the Seventh Line celebrated by organizing an ice fishing expedition in the Persephone Township Moose Bus, with Freddy at the wheel. Constable Bradley pulled them over for speeding, belching smoke and impersonating a school bus. And Pookie didn't change. He still harbours bloodthirsty designs on Willy's lower regions. But that didn't stop Willy from asking Isobel out to the Ice Storm Dance for the Heart and Stroke Fund. He got her a costume as the Ice Princess, and he went as her knight in shining armour.

Walt said he'd never suspected Willy had such a sense of romance. But Freddy said, "It isn't the romance, Walt, it's the tin pants."

INFERNO

Another note from the editor:
I just received a letter from our insurance company, advising me of a hefty hike in our premiums. They offered only this by way of explanation:

Dear Sir,
     Please be advised that we are reviewing your insurance coverage in light of the increased risk factors that are associated with running a weekly newspaper.

     It's odd, because I thought the weekly newspaper business was getting safer. In this country we haven't lost a printing press to violent insurrection since 1826. That was the year a bunch of hooligans destroyed the newspaper office of that radical, William Lyon Mackenzie. Even then, a jury awarded damages to Mackenzie, which helped him set up shop again, made him famous and enabled him to start an insurrection of his very own ten years later.
     Turns out the "risk factors" this fellow is talking about have nothing to do with violence or property damage. He's just trying to protect himself after the McKelvey incident. Dry Cry McKelvey is the skinflint who runs the general

store and building supply in Larkspur. Last winter a big national outfit set up shop outside of town with the slogan "We've got your lumber." "Not for long, you don't," said Dry Cry and set out in the dead of night to torch the place. But it had just snowed, and he slipped on the handicapped access ramp. The snow put out his torch, and the fall put out his back. So he sued the company for not exercising due diligence in snow removal. He won and now the insurance company thinks all our premiums should go up.

We're not all Dry Crys in this community, but try explaining that to an insurance company. I figured I'd check with Walt. If anyone knows anything about managing risk, it would be him. He's been juggling the farm, his work at the brokerage firm and, for the last nine months, a baby.

September 21

Dear Ed,

My biggest problem these days is sleep deprivation. I've always been sympathetic to those new fathers sitting in the Monday morning meetings with that thousand-yard stare. Now I know how it feels—it's brutal.

The other day my partner, Alf Harrison, said that he thinks I came back from maternity leave too soon. I wondered what gave him that idea. He said that I drifted off during the Comco Pension Fund meeting, so he gave me a nudge and said it was "my turn." Apparently I picked up his cellphone and told him I was going to warm it up then we could all "go sleepy-bye-byes."

It's not the actual sleeping time. It's the sleep interruption that plays havoc with your circadian rhythms. Hope gets a lot of colds, and every time they go straight to her ears. We have some drops for her, but the only thing that gives her effective relief is yelling for about an hour.

But a couple of weeks ago we passed a milestone. Maggie finally broke down and left Hope in the hands of someone else for the evening. For the first time in nine months, we went out on a date. Gertrude Lynch was wonderfully helpful during Maggie's confinement, and when I called she said she was happy to babysit.

"But you know you'll have to get rid of that dog, Walt," she warned.

"Spike?" I asked, somewhat taken aback.

"He isn't safe around the baby. You know what they say: 'The house is filled with perils untold, when the child is new and the dog is old.'"

The vet warned me about this, too. But Spike has been with me almost from the beginning here. He was originally Freddy's dog, but there were problems. He wandered, he chased deer, he stayed out all night, and finally Spike just couldn't stand it anymore. One day he followed me home, and he's been here ever since.

But, of course, a baby changes everything. Animal psychologists say it's because the dog suddenly finds itself no longer the centre of attention. It gets jealous and may eventually even attack the child. But Spike's always been so gentle. I asked Maggie about it while we were doing dishes.

"Have you ever known dogs to attack babies?"

"It doesn't come up, Walt. Where I come from, dogs live outside. Right next to the barn they have a nice, cozy doghouse, which they have to share with the husband from time to time. But they don't seem to mind."

Maggie has never warmed to the idea of an inside dog, although I remember two beagles named Amos and Andy that Freddy attempted to housetrain while Maggie was still living with him. For quite a while I thought their names were Geddoff and Geddout.

"I know you're fond of Spike, dear, but it's a real question," said Maggie. "Hope's starting to get pretty mobile. We can't watch her every second."

I sat down on the floor and had a heart-to-heart chat with Spike over his supper bowl.

"Look, old bean," I said. "I know I've been busy and we haven't got out as much as we used to. And I guess I've been preoccupied and missed a couple of doggie supper times. But you wouldn't hold that against Hope, would you?"

Spike looked at me with those mournful eyes and said, "Woof."

The trouble is, I don't know what woof means. So I decided I'd better just keep an eye on him.

Anyway, when we got back from our date, I checked in with Mrs. Lynch on the verandah while Maggie was inside, crooning over a sleeping Hope.

"How did you manage?" I asked her.

"I managed, Walt. But I was right. You'll have to get rid of that dog. That's an accident just waiting to happen."

I didn't say anything to Maggie but I kept a close eye on Spike and Hope for the next few days. Then, last night, we went out again. This time Freddy came down to babysit. As soon as we got home and shut off the engine we could hear it from right across the yard—Hope howling, Freddy shouting, Spike woofing. We rushed inside and found Hope standing red-faced in her playpen. Freddy and Spike were glaring at each other in the middle of the room. You could cut the tension with a knife.

Freddy's shoulders dropped with relief when he saw us. "Jeez, am I glad to see to see you guys!" he said, "Welcome to Fight Night."

Maggie scooped Hope up in her arms and soothed her. "There, there, darling. What's the matter?" she cooed. Then she turned on Freddy. "What is the matter with her! What happened here?"

Freddy shrugged. "I reckon she's probably hungry after all this time."

"Didn't you feed her? We left the formula in the fridge for you."

"Feed her?" sputtered Freddy. "I couldn't get anywhere near her. Spike wouldn't let me."

Apparently Spike only said what he always says— "woof." But in this case woof meant, "If you want to touch the kid, you go through me."

Freddy watched Spike retire to his corner and flop down, exhausted.

"That dog's been on the job all night," he said. "Never moved once. If Hope had the St. John's Ambulance and the Secret Service looking after her, she wouldn't be any safer than she is with that dog."

So I guess we don't have to worry about Spike being jealous. I've been watching the two of them this past week. There's starting to be a little bare spot in Spike's fur behind his left ear. It's where Hope hangs on to him as they roam around the house.

Hope makes a lot of little sounds, and we're perched on the edge of our seats, waiting for her first word. I must confess I've been campaigning at mealtimes with her favourite raspberry Jell-O to get her to say "daddy" first. I hold a spoon just a few inches from her mouth, look her directly in the eye and say, "Da da da da! Can you say that, Hope? Da da? Can you say 'daddy'?"

Maggie caught me at it today.

"That's not fair," she complained, and sat down on the other side of Hope's chair. "'Daddy' is easier to say than 'mummy.' But you can say it, can't you, darling? Say 'mum mum...mummy'!"

"Da da...daddy!"

"Mum mum...mummy!"

Hope looked from Maggie to me and back again. Then she gave a little hiccup and said quite clearly: "'pike!"

Lots of babies have been raised by animals: Mowgli by wolves, Tarzan by the apes. Rumour has it that Dry Cry McKelvey was brought up by turkey vultures.

Yours sincerely,
Walt

October 15

Dear Ed,

Now that I'm a family man, I thought I should have a look at disability insurance. You know, $5,000 if you lose a hand, $10,000 for an eye, $25,000 for an arm and a leg... cheerful stuff. And, if you prefer not to dispose of yourself bit by bit, there's always accidental death. That particular "black hole" is worth more than the sum of your parts.

I still have a disability policy at the firm, but I thought it should be updated. So this week I had lunch with the insurance guy we always deal with in the city. He promised to write something up, but he warned me that it would involve major changes.

"You're on the farm now, Walt," he explained. "If we write a new policy, I'd have to move you into a new classification. Right now you're A-2 Office Worker—pretty low risk."

My office staff is low risk all right. I hardly ever see them move. I wondered what kind of worker could be considered A-1. Probably senators.

"So, what classification am I now?" I asked.

He riffled through his black book. "Let's see…it looks like you'd be F-18. That's parachute testers, bomb defusers and farmers. And fighter pilots. It's more expensive."

He wasn't sure how much more, but he'll let me know. I expect it'll be considerably more, because, for the first time ever, he bought lunch.

I was curious about all this, so I went down to see Don. He and Freddy were having a coffee break on his verandah. Freddy wouldn't carry a nickel of insurance, but I figured that since Don has a wife and three kids, he would probably have some kind of plan that would work for me.

"If you don't mind my asking, what do you pay for disability insurance?" I asked.

"Nothin'," said Don. "Can't afford it. And I don't know who can. I keep a bit of life insurance through the federation, and I take out crop insurance most years, but my real insurance is those seven guys out there."

He waved at the neighbouring farms dotted around the slopes of the Pine River Valley.

"I know if I get laid up and can't get the crop off, those fellas will be on my fields tomorrow. And they know I'd do the same for them."

"Yep," said Freddy. "Count on your neighbours, Walt. You're better off to stick with your old policy, the one with the Office Worker classification. Then, if you get hurt bad, we'll drag you inside the house and drop a filing cabinet on you. Hey, what are friends for?"

I was pondering this on the train home from the city. The trip offers more time for reflection than it used to, because the last twenty miles cross about a dozen bridges and culverts that have been downgraded to a fifteen-mile-an-hour limit—for insurance reasons, of course. This drops the average speed of the trip to thirty miles an hour, which is actually one mile an hour slower than when the line was built in 1856.

It was still light when the spires of Larkspur appeared on the horizon. While I was away, the fall plowing had begun, turning the fields of the Pine River Valley to slabs of chocolate. Combines munched through cornfields, billowing dark clouds of dust behind them. I stepped off the train and breathed in the smells of home: ripe apples, freshly turned earth and burning leaves. I had a few minutes to spare before Maggie picked me up, so I sat down on the war memorial in front of the station to enjoy the evening. A light ring of white mist surrounded the Orange Hall like a halo. Little plumes of it steamed out of the vents under the eaves. With a start, I realized that the Orange Hall was on fire!

Fortunately, our 911 service has recently been upgraded. I grabbed my cellphone and dialled. A voice promptly responded.

"Hello?" I said. "The Orange Hall is on fire...No, I don't know the numerical fire code, but you know the building—it's at the four corners of Wellington Street and the Town Li...well, it used to be the Town Line. Now it's Regional Road number...oh, what is it..."

"What town is that, sir?"

"Right in Larkspur."

"And where is Larkspur?"

"Larkspur? It's north of Highway 13, about five miles west of Demeter—"

"And what province is that, sir?"

"In Ontario, for Pete's sake! Where are you?"

At that moment the 4×4 swung into the parking lot and Maggie jumped out.

"Walt, I need to use the phone," she said and took it from me. She dialled seven numbers and had to wait only a few seconds. "Sparky," she said into the phone. "The Orange Hall's on fire! Get the boys!" Then she handed it back to me. "Well, this is a fine how-do-you-do," she sighed.

"Thank goodness you got here. Who knows how long it would have taken me to give directions to someone coming from Nova Scotia."

"Well, the volunteers are on their way, but I don't know if it'll help much," said Maggie. "You know what we call the fire department, Walt—the Larkspur Basement Savers."

I've heard this before. Don't get me wrong; the Larkspur Volunteers are a great group. No matter what the weather, they are on the scene within minutes. They train and fundraise relentlessly. But still, their success rate isn't all that good. Let's just say their save percentage wouldn't keep them playing goal in the NHL. They're more in the league of the Ancient Mariner, who, you may recall, "stoppeth one of three."

The fire truck skidded to a halt in front of the hall. Sparky McKeown leapt from the cab, barking orders in all directions. Sparky has been the fire chief for years and years. In fact, he's been chief for so long no one can remember when they started calling him Sparky. He has lots of experience fighting fires. The trouble is, quite a few of them have been on his own farm. The drive shed went first, then the dairy barn, then the house. There were the usual rumours. As Freddy put it, "Try as you like, you cannot save old farm buildings by loadin' them up with insurance."

Anyway, I don't think anyone could have saved the Orange Hall—it was too far gone. The volunteers did what they could to contain the fire. They hooked up hoses and soon had two streams arcing through the air. Two men actually went into the building for a few brief minutes and came out again, one carrying a large painting of William the Third crossing the Boyne River, the other following with an armful of brightly coloured flags from the Regalia Room. Gertrude Lynch, whose house is right next door to the hall came and stood beside us.

"Why are they rescuing that junk?" she complained. "What about the piano?"

"It's too far back," said Maggie. "The floor might collapse under them."

As she spoke, there was an ominous crack, then a sickening crash as the piano hit the bowling alley in the basement. Two hundred and twenty strings of piano wire gave up the ghost with a sound like an original composition by R. Murray Schafer. Then the steel roofing at the rear buckled and an angry spike of orange flame shot up through the gap. A window exploded and the curls of white smoke along the eaves changed to thick black clouds. I heard a sound like an engine revving up and realized it was air rushing in through the window to feed the fire. The two spouts of water shifted away from the hall and began playing on Gertrude's house. One brave soul remained on a ladder against the front of the hall, prying off the wooden sign that read LOL Number 26, Larkspur 1954.

The Orange Hall was burning down. Scenes from the last five years flashed across my mind: Old Jimmy step-dancing under the chestnut tree in the dark. The Price Family Orchestra playing all night with babies in baskets parked along the edge of the stage in front of them. Our wedding dance was here. We were at the Berry Festival Dance when Maggie told me she was pregnant. She gave birth to Hope in the Regalia Room. And it was all going up in a whirl of flame.

"The lights have been on in this hall every night for fifty years. It's going to leave a big hole," said Maggie quietly.

"Well, I guess, thank goodness for insurance, after all," I said.

Maggie looked at me. "It's the Orange Lodge, Walt. It's not insured."

Shadows and emergency lights played on the sea of faces staring at the collapsing building. Not a person spoke. Gertrude Lynch stood on the front walk of her house and dabbed at her eyes with a handkerchief. Finally, Maggie touched my arm.

"C'mon, Walt. Let's go home."

Yours sincerely,
Walt

October 20

Dear Ed,

King is my oldest horse; I bought him from Freddy four years ago, and he was ready to retire back then. I don't know exactly how old King is, but people often comment about the deep worry lines on his face. I tell them it's because he remembers the Cuban Missile Crisis.

I don't know how old Feedbin and Mortgage are either, but they are very long in the tooth. You tell a horse's age by looking at its teeth. As the horse ages, the front teeth get longer and the back teeth are worn down to almost nothing. It's the opposite of how you tell the age of a hockey player.

Old they may be; slow they are not. The first season was a nightmare, trying to work up the little field in front of the house. It was like water-skiing behind a boat with no driver. My neighbour across the road, the Squire, came over one morning to make an observation in my very first year on the farm, just a few months after I first met him.

"I was looking at the big circles in your crop from my bedroom window and thought maybe you were getting visits from alien spaceships," he said.

"No, it's just the horses," I said. "When they take off, they always do a big circle in the field and head back to the barn. I'd like to teach them to make sharper turns, but first I'd have to get them to go a bit slower."

"You need a bigger space to work in . . . like Saskatchewan," he chuckled.

"Is there a bigger field where I could practise?" I asked.

"I've got that twenty-five acres across the road. Maybe you'd like to rent it?" he offered.

"I don't know. There sure are a lot of stones on it."

"You gotta have the stones, Walt. They knock the dirt off the implements when you're goin' around the field."

"Oh," I said. "I didn't know that. But I notice on Calvin Currie's fields the stones are all in piles."

"Yeah, Calvin just got them in last week. He hasn't got them spread yet."

The horses never really did settle down, and I came to regard the whole investment as a dead loss. Then, out of the blue, Feedbin had a secret affair and produced a filly. Somewhat hopefully, I named her Dividend. She seems to be a natural pacer, and I made a brief attempt at training her to harness with an old two-wheeled buggy I got from the Mennonites. I took her out on the unopened road allowance at the end of the Seventh Line, where I thought we would be fairly safe. But she got going so fast I couldn't hold her, and we sliced off a row of mailboxes trying to negotiate the turn onto the 25 Sideroad. One of the mailboxes belonged to a guy from Alberta—a big, tall man with a moustache and a Stetson. I was helping him set up a new mailbox the next day when he made an observation about Dividend.

"You know, I can help you put some brains in that horse if you want to leave her with me some afternoon. She'd be a lot safer to handle."

"Oh, really?" I said. "What can you do in an afternoon?"

"I can explain to her what we mean out west when we say 'whoa'."

When I asked him about his technique for working with a problem horse, he talked about a second set of reins and a surcingle and a running martingale down through the thingummies...Now, I know about reins and bridles, but when people start talking about surcingles and martingales, they might as well be speaking medieval Italian to me. However, the man seemed to know what he was doing, so one day I led Dividend over and left her with him. When I picked her up that evening, she was a changed horse. I could lead her around with a piece of string. If the buggy ever comes back from the Mennonite repair shop in Elmira, I think I might try her in harness again.

In the meantime, she still enjoys a breakout. Last week Maggie was going to let me sleep in after my stint in the city. But she appeared at the top of the stairs shortly after seven and announced that Dividend was joyriding again, out on the road.

Dividend's breakouts all follow the same pattern. She goes to the south end of the road allowance and waits; when I show up in the 4×4, the chase is on, back to the barn. Sure enough, as soon as she saw the 4×4, her tail went up and she took off out onto the road. She's amazing to watch like this. It's like she's on a set of tracks. Her whole body stretches out and the dirt flies out behind her as she hammers down the road. And she never breaks into a canter. This morning she was really humming, and when we got back to the farm she shot right past the gate without even glancing at it, and then right past Freddy's gate, too. That left nothing between her and the highway. I stepped on the gas, got out in front of her and honked the horn until she ran down into the ditch and turned around. She whinnied cheerfully and pounded off back down the Seventh Line. I was relieved to see Freddy standing at his gate this time, but he didn't stop her. He just stood there and watched as we flashed by. I stepped on the gas, chased her down once more and got her turned around.

This time, Freddy waved her in. She streaked down the lane to the barnyard past the drive shed, where Freddy and Maggie's two nephews, Willy and Dave, were repairing a giant corn picker. They both looked up as Dividend went past, and Dave trotted over to swing the barnyard gate shut.

"You don't normally see something going that fast without slicks and a brake chute," he said.

Freddy walked over. "Did you see her out there, fellas?" he asked. "Three times the length of the concession, and look at her. She wouldn't blow out a candle."

"Look at the ass-end on her," agreed Willy. "Where you been hiding this one, Walt?"

"This is Feedbin's filly," I replied.

"Feedbin's filly, huh?" said Dave. "That's where this one gets her speed, then."

"Apparently, Feedbin wasn't that fast," I said. "I understand she was retired after one season."

"Oh, she was fast enough," said Dave. "Feedbin had all the speed in the world. The problem was, she always broke stride. You see, in harness racing, if a horse breaks into a canter, it has to pull over and yield to other horses until it gets back on stride. Most horses have to be trained not to break stride, but some have the gene that makes them natural pacers, and they're worth their weight in gold. So, who was the father to this one?"

It was anybody's guess, but I always suspected a scruffy black stallion that Freddy brought home from the track during my first year on the farm. He got out a few times.

"E-mail?" said Dave. "Well, that explains it, then. His

great-great-great grandfather was one of the great natural pacers in this part of the world—Clipper Ship."

"Oh, yeah," agreed Freddy. "That was the start of a breeding line where every generation seemed to get a little bit faster than the one before. What was the colt they got out of Clipper Ship?"

"Pony Express," said Willy. "And then Pony Express sired Overnight Courier."

"Yeah that's right," said Freddy. "And then Overnight Courier begat Telegram. And Telegram begat Fax Machine, who begat E-mail, who begat . . . Say, Walt, we need a racing name for this filly. Jeez, what goes faster than e-mail?"

"I don't know," I said. "How about Paycheque? Gone before you see it."

Dave stroked Dividend's neck admiringly. He gave me a sideways look and said, "Say, Walt. Why don't you leave her up here with us for a bit? She's got a lot of jam, and she needs someone to work with her. Preferably someone with no dependants."

That was fine with me. Dave has this way with animals. If St. Francis of Assisi were a dirtbike racer—that'd be Dave. A few days later I bumped into him outside the post office in Larkspur and he looked preoccupied.

"How's the training going?" I asked.

"Awful, Walt," he said. "I can't figure it out. When you put the bridle on her, she just stands there and shakes. Did she have something bad happen to her? Any train wrecks when you had her out?"

I said, "Just the business with the mailboxes. And she was going so fast that time I don't think she even noticed."

Dave mulled this over. "Anybody else work with her?"

"That guy from Alberta; he had a few hours with her teaching her how to stop."

Dave nodded. "Oh, yeah, the Mountain Man. What did he do?"

I tried to explain the harness arrangement as if I knew what I was talking about: the second set of reins that went through the bellyband and the running martingale...

"A Flyin' W!" cried Dave in horror.

"A Flying W—that's what he called it. Why, what's the matter? What is that, anyway?"

Dave winced. "Jeez, Walt. Those reins don't go to her mouth, they go down to her front feet. If the horse runs away and doesn't stop when you say whoa, you yank her front feet out from under her and knock her flat on her face."

"Oh, my goodness, that's awful!" I said. "He told me he was just going to make her safe."

"Well, she's safe, all right," said Dave, shaking his head. "She's so safe she don't know what she's for anymore. Jeez, Walt, I can't believe you did a 'Flying W' on a filly from the line of the great Clipper Ship."

And with that he walked away to his truck.

Yours sincerely,
Walt

October 27

Dear Ed,

This hasn't been a good week for livestock. After the business with Dividend, I noticed that our egg production had dropped drastically. I went down to the barn one day last week and looked in all the usual places, but there wasn't a single one. I asked Maggie if she thought maybe the short nights and the cooler weather would make them stop laying.

"No," she said. "Nothing's wrong with the hens, Walt. We've got a thief, one with four feet. My guess is that it's a skunk."

"I thought security was pretty tight in here. So, I guess I should get one those wire traps from the Humane Society, huh? Would that work for a skunk?"

"Yes, it would trap the skunk," she agreed. "Then what?"

"Then I take it somewhere far away and release it, right?"

"Not if you want to sleep in the house," she said.

"Ah, yes...I see."

I love challenges like this. It's like those case studies they put in front of you at business school to test your skill at problem solving. I made my own humane trap, consisting of a long smooth board, a tall sawhorse, an egg and a garbage can. The board was hinged like a seesaw at the sawhorse, and I fixed an egg to the end of the board with an elastic band. As the candidate stepped out to the end of the board, it would tip, and he would slide down into the garbage can, which, of course, has a lid. I set it up.

Next morning I checked it out. The trap was sprung. But there was no candidate. The garbage can was lying on its side and the egg was gone. It was a skunk all right. The aroma hanging in the air told me that it had fired a warning shot at the garbage can.

But I don't give up easily. I was confident I could think my way through this. I just needed to find a way to

temporarily immobilize the skunk. Horse tranquilizer! I'll
inject horse tranquilizer into the egg. It works fast. The
skunk gets the egg, falls into the trap and then just goes to
sleep. I went to the vet to get some.

"What would you use it for, Mr. Wingfield?" asked the
doctor. I explained my plan while he listened with one eyebrow raised. When I finished, he thought for a moment.

"It's an interesting approach," he conceded. "It should
tranquilize the skunk, all right. Then what?"

"Then I take it out to the escarpment somewhere and
dump it. What do you think?"

"You could do that," he said. "But you don't want to be
too long about it. This stuff is time-specific. You've got five
hours, at the most, before the skunk wakes up—scared and
mad."

Five hours seemed like plenty of time. I just had to
know exactly when the trap was sprung. And that part was
easy. I'd just sit up in the barn until I heard a kerfuffle and a
thump. I filled a syringe with horse tranquilizer and
injected two eggs with it, since I might have need of a
backup—and trundled off to put my plan to the test.

So, that's how I came to be sitting motionless in a dark
corner of the barn on a very pleasant Saturday evening in
late October, waiting for the sound of a homemade skunk
trap being blundered into. I really didn't mind the waiting.
It was such a pleasant Saturday evening, unusually pleasant
for late October. And, anyway, it gave me a chance to think
about stuff. I got a letter from my insurance company
telling me that they don't insure farms and that I have to
find another carrier. My broker tells me this is happening a
lot these days. He said I was lucky, because some farmers

can't be insured at all. It's too expensive. The Orange Lodge couldn't afford it. More and more low-income home owners and even drivers are just doing without it. Who's to blame? Who's the skunk here?

You can't really blame the insurance companies. If people are going to sue for damages when a cup of coffee spills in their laps—well, the money's got to come from somewhere. And no matter what you want to say about lawyers—and who doesn't?—it's not really their fault. They're just representing the interests of their clients.

So who is the skunk? Is it the courts who award the damages? Is that why judges are all in black with those white collars and stripey things? Sitting in the gloom of the barn, listening to soft rock on the talk-free FM station, was making my mind wander.

I glanced at my watch. It was three o'clock in the morning and my eyes were starting to close. Maybe tonight wasn't the night. I started to think maybe I should have a little nap. It looked as if we might not get any action this night, anyway, and it couldn't hurt if I just rested my eyes for a bit, even just for a few minutes. I made my way up to the house in the dark, let myself in quietly and stretched out on the sofa.

When I woke up, it was getting light outside. I grabbed the remote and turned on the television. It was 7:05. I'd slept for four hours! I pulled my boots on and trotted back down to the barn. It was beautiful outside. The morn in russet mantle clad walks o'er the dew of Calvin Currie's pasture. A really lovely late-October Sunday morning.

Better yet, the trap was sprung, the egg was gone, and the skunk was in the garbage can, sleeping peacefully. This was okay. The earliest this could have happened was three in the morning. That still gave me an hour. I reached in, grasped the skunk gently but firmly by the scruff and lifted it out of the garbage can.

The thing I had forgotten is that on a Saturday night in late October, everywhere in Canada—except in Saskatchewan—we change over from daylight saving to standard time by moving our clocks...

The skunk woke up.

Skunks have only one natural defence. But it's a beauty. That night I slept in the barn. But Maggie was very sweet. Next morning she came out to the barn, with a clothespin on her nose, and brought me breakfast—warm toast and a lovely soft-boiled egg, just the way I like it...

Of course, she used the other egg. I'm pretty sure it was an accident. I made it out of the barn as far as the horse feeder and then decided it was time for another nap. This time, I got about ten hours of the most restful sleep I have ever known.

Yours sincerely,
Walt

November 5

Dear Ed,

There's an old rock elm stump in my lower pasture that has been rotting very slowly since the elm blight swept through this area forty years ago. Snows cover it in winter; wild grape vines and scotch thistles shroud it from view during the summer. But in the melt and frost of the shoulder seasons, it emerges pretty much unchanged, stubbornly refusing to rot down and disappear. I was reminded of that stump this week when I paid a visit to the offices of our local regional government of Hillview.

The recent restructuring of the old township councils into a regional government created a lot of upset, partly because so many councillors, clerks and road crew were declared redundant and bounced out of their jobs. People like Harold MacNabb, the man who has served as Persephone Township's clerk-treasurer, Fair Board secretary and bartender at the Legion since . . . well, since before Mackenzie King was born.

Anyway, a week after the fire, I got a call came from the secretary to the Chief Administrative Officer for Hillview, inviting me to a meeting to discuss the rebuilding plans for the Orange Hall. It was my first visit to the new admin centre on Wellington Street—an air-conditioned chrome and glass tower that really stands out. On the third floor, the secretary ushered me into a large, handsomely decorated office. A figure in a leather armchair was talking on the phone with his back to me. As I entered, the chair swung around to reveal Nine Lives Harold, the old clerk of Persephone.

"Well, now, Mr. Wingfield. Won't you sit down?"

I was so startled I forgot to congratulate him on his appointment.

"Very good of you to take the time to see me, Mr. Wingfield," said Harold. "I know you're a busy man, so I'll come right to the point. Your name has come forward as a candidate for the steering committee to rebuild the Orange Hall. Council has instructed me to ascertain if you'd be willing to serve."

"They have?" I asked in surprise.

I have crossed paths with Harold twice before, and on both occasions I went home empty-handed, with a vague sensation of having been blindsided by a Ministry of Transportation snowplow.

"Why would they want me for the committee?" I asked cautiously.

"In point of fact, we was thinking of you for chairman."

"Chairman! I don't know what to say..."

"We were hoping you would say yes. The committee needs someone with a solid understanding of finance and the expertise to run a public building campaign. Clearly, you possess both. So, what do you think?"

"Well, I'm flattered to be asked," I stammered. "It's a very worthwhile project and a great challenge..."

"A challenge? Oh, it is that," he agreed warmly.

"When would we start?" I asked.

"That would be your call, Mr. Chairman."

I hadn't actually said yes, but by the time I got to the elevator I seemed to have lost the opportunity to say no. When I arrived home, Hope was sitting on Freddy's lap on the verandah, a watchful Spike close by. Freddy was instructing Hope in the art of calling wild turkeys.

"Can't start 'em too soon, Walt," he said cheerfully. "Those turkeys are great eatin' when they're barbequed. You gotta get a young one, though."

"Oh," I said. "I guess the old ones are pretty tough, are they?"

"No, they're good eatin' too. But the old ones generally have a computer chip planted just here under the wing. And those game wardens will track you right to your freezer. Always remember that, Hope."

I told him about being appointed chairman. Freddy frowned.

"Jeez, Walt, isn't that kinda public? I got a fieldstone foundation wall at the back of my barn. You could bang your head against that for as long as you like and no one need know but you and the cows."

Freddy has always been a cynic when it comes to public service. At that moment we looked up to see Don mounting the steps of the verandah.

"You guys doin' coffee here?" he asked.

"Maybe something stronger," said Freddy. "Guess who Harold just nabbed to chair the new Orange Hall Building Committee."

Don has actually served on council. I knew I'd get a more measured response from him.

"Did he pull a gun on you, Walt?"

Just at that moment Maggie drove in with a load of groceries. Freddy handed Hope to me and scampered down the steps to help her with the bags.

"Let me take a couple of those, Maggie," he said. "Maybe the chairman here could get the apple juice."

Maggie glanced up at me. "Yes, I heard," she said. "It's all over town."

"Well, what do you think?" I asked.

She straightened up and paused. "Well, I'm just surprised, that's all," she said. "You've always been perfectly nice to him."

"Oh, come on, people," I said. "It's easy to be cynical, but lots of committees work just fine, and, you know, they *can* get things done. They just have to be run properly, that's all."

Maggie tossed Freddy two bags of diapers. "If the fence needs painting," she said, "give me a paintbrush and let me paint the fence. But don't expect me to sit through a meeting of the Fair Board and talk all night about how we're going to paint the fence. It just puts me out of temper." And she breezed past me into the house.

However, she allowed the appointment to stand. I convened the first meeting of the Steering Committee at the home of Gertrude Lynch, since she's also on the committee and lives right next door to the site. A little before eight last Tuesday night, I tapped on Gertrude's door. I was a few minutes early, but I found the committee already assembled around Gertrude's arborite kitchen table. Harold rose, smiling his affable smile, and shook my hand.

"We'll put you right here, Mr. Wingfield...that is, Mr. Chairman." And he ushered me to the chair at the end of the table. Besides Gertrude and myself, there are two other committee members—those former township councillors who were so interested and unhelpful with my museum proposal—Ernie and Wilfrid. They also happen to be the last two Orangemen in the community. Ernie's been president of the Fair Board, the Federation of Agriculture, Soil and Crop, the Plowmen's, the Curling Club...they say that during his lifetime he has run for everything except cover.

"Evening, Mr. Wingfield," boomed Ernie. He always talks to you as though you're at the other end of a hayfield.

Wilfrid is the secretary of the Orange Lodge. Judging by his age, he could write much of the lodge's history in Canada from personal experience.

"Evening, Mr. Windfall," he croaked, not attempting to get out his chair.

"Wingfield," I corrected him.

Wilfrid looked at Ernie. "What did he say?"

"WingFIELD," repeated Gertrude.

"Oh, I feel fine, thank you," said Wilfrid.

I let the matter pass and brought the meeting to order.

"First, I'd like to thank you all for agreeing to accept this challenge," I said. "Tonight is going to be a fact-finding exercise, and I'm going to get right down to business, but—"

"Don't need to spend much time on it," announced Ernie flatly. "Just bulldoze the place and put up a couple of nice bungalows."

"Well, sure . . ." I said as patiently as I could. "That's one possibility, but we're here to explore a range of opportunities. I want to pass something around the table that I found in the township archives yesterday."

I showed them a photograph of the lodge building under construction just about fifty years ago. It's a wonderful picture. There must be fifty people assembled on and around the building, all of them grinning from ear to ear and just so pleased with themselves. You can tell how proud they are of what they accomplished.

As it passed around, I said, "Imagine what it must have felt like, creating something like that from nothing."

"I know what it felt like, Mr. Wingfield," said Harold, "because I was on that committee. That's me there—the handsome young fella at the front. I guess Wilfrid might have worked on the committee, too, but you were already retired, weren't you, Wilfrid?"

"What's that?" said Wilfrid, his eyes snapping open.

"Battery's gone on his hearing aid," said Ernie. He leaned over to Wilfrid's ear. "NEVER MIND, WILFRID. WE'LL TELL YOU WHICH WAY TO VOTE." Then he put his finger on the picture. "That's my dad, there. He hauled the cement up from the train station with a wagon and a team of horses. Worked for more than a month and never got a cent out of it, unlike some people."

This remark jolted Gertrude upright in her chair. "If you're referring to my father," she said, "he did all the finish carpentry, but the only money he took was the cost of hinges and doorknobs."

Ernie snorted. "He tarted the place up, using money we didn't have for stuff we didn't need."

"There was provision in the budget for cupboards," said Gertrude.

"The budget was for hooks and shelves. My dad always said you don't need cupboards if you have nothing to hide. There were more doors and hinges in that place than in a New Orleans cathouse!"

"You have the advantage of me there, Ernie," said Gertrude evenly. "I've never been in a New Orleans cathouse. And your father couldn't be expected to understand the need for cupboards, because he was born in a barn—"

"Now, now," I said, leaning between the two of them. "We're not here to dig up old feuds and reopen old wounds. Come on, people, a plague on both your houses!"

"What did he say?" asked Wilfrid.

Ernie turned to him. "I dunno. SOMETHING ABOUT BOTH OUR HOUSES!"

Wilfrid nodded happily. "Well, I agree . . . a couple of nice bungalows."

"Look," I said. "We're rushing the fences here. Our first task tonight should be to establish exactly what our resources are. What is the financial position of the lodge? Can either of the lodge members speak to that?"

"What did he say?" asked Wilfrid.

"DOES THE LODGE HAVE ANY MONEY?"

"Oh, sure," said Wilfrid. "When I went to the bank two weeks ago, there was $361.96. It'll be higher now with the interest paid since then."

"Well, I knew we'd have to fundraise," I sighed. "Just makes the job a little more challenging. We'll have to get a mortgage of some kind. All right, then, apart from finances, are there any other obstacles we might face?"

Harold raised a finger and said, "Can't build on the lot as it is."

"Oh," I said. "Why is that?"

"It's too small for today's regulations. It would have to be rezoned."

I made a note of that. "Okay," I said. "We've got to finance the entire amount and apply for rezoning. Anything else?"

Harold's finger went up again. "The insurance company will have some concerns."

"But I thought there was no insurance."

Harold shrugged. "You can't get a mortgage if it's not insured. And they won't give us insurance unless we put in a new septic tank."

I added the septic system to the list. "Is that it?" I asked, glancing automatically at Harold's finger. It twitched again.

"They'll want a new well," he said apologetically. "And a paved parking lot with lighting, stormwater drainage and, of course, handicapped access."

It went like that all evening. By ten o'clock it was time to sum up. It appeared that, to satisfy the requirements of the bank, the township and the insurance company, we were looking at spending about a million dollars altogether. After I said this figure out loud, a dead silence hung over the room. It appeared that any enthusiasm that might have come into the room earlier that evening was rapidly draining away. An injection of energy and optimism was urgently needed.

"I know that looks like a daunting sum," I said, "but the trick is to break it down into smaller chunks—then it all looks more manageable. For instance, from each man, woman and child in the community it comes to only..." I did a rapid calculation on my pocket calculator. "Let's see...ten thousand dollars each." The silence deepened and I plunged on.

"The important thing is not to get discouraged. You know, five hundred years ago, the people of Florence in Renaissance Italy had a town square, and it had a tall tower with a huge bell nicknamed the Cowbell. Whenever something really important happened, the Cowbell rang and all the people would come down to the square to hear the news and decide what they were going to do. Our modern democratic system has its roots in that town square in Florence. People gathered there to debate the big issues and to vote in their leaders. They held festivals there with food and games and entertainment.

"That's what the Orange Hall is to us. It defines us as a people just as surely as that town square defined the Florentines. And it is just as vital a community resource. Don't you see how important it is?"

I could see them nodding to each other, and I leaned back in my chair. It appeared that I was reaching them.

"We're agreed, then," said Ernie.

"Well, thank goodness," I grinned at him. "I think we've made a start."

Ernie shook his head. "No, I didn't mean you...I'm saying we agree with him." He waved at Wilfrid, who stirred to life once again.

"Yeah, I think we should bulldoze the place and put up a couple of nice bungalows."

I drove home in the dark. It had turned chilly and the wind was wild. It whipped up swirling towers of dead leaves in the headlights, and the clouds sailed like ghostly galleons above me. I was still talking to myself when I walked in the door at home. Maggie and Freddy were sitting in front of the fire. Hope had an earache again, and she was fussing.

"She won't settle," said Maggie, handing Hope to me. "Let me sleep for a couple of hours, will you, and then I'll take over again. Freddy, would you stay and visit with Walt? Someone will have to talk him down after his committee meeting."

She went upstairs and Freddy went over to my liquor cabinet.

"So, you look like you've been wading through the tar pits," he said cheerfully.

I just shook my head in exasperation. "Do you know anything about Dante's *Inferno*?" I asked him.

"Is that the new pizza place in Port Petunia?"

"Well, it's Italian," I laughed. "But it's not a restaurant. It's a book, a very long poem about a trip that a man takes through the nine circles of Hell."

"You have had a rough night," said Freddy. "Can I pour you something?"

"A couple of fingers, thanks. When the pilgrim finds his way down to the seventh circle, he sees all the tortured souls stretched out on the burning sand, swatting away at the flames and complaining about the heat. Then he recognizes the faces of people he knows: moneylenders, stockbrokers and insurance agents. He asks his guide what makes these people such terrible sinners. And he's told that it is God's will for man to make his living through creativity and industry...from the sweat of his brow. These people make their living off the creativity and industry of others. Worse than that, by doing so, they stifle human achievement."

Freddy clinked glasses with me. "Stifling creativity is this country's biggest growth industry," he said. "If that's what the seventh circle is for, they're gonna have to build an addition onto it."

"I suppose. The thing is, fifty years ago, it would have been perfectly simple to gather up building supplies, muster the will of the community and just rebuild the Orange Hall. But now, at every turn, there's some new constraint that adds to the costs, and it adds and it adds until you simply can't do it anymore. We're paralyzed. We're trapped in the seventh circle of the Inferno."

"Well, with winter coming on, I guess there's worse places to be," said Freddy.

"Yeah, but remember what it said over the gate at the entrance to Hell: 'Abandon hope, all ye who enter here.'"

Hope sighed and blinked slowly. It looked like half my audience was about to nod off.

"No one's going to abandon you, Hope. Not while I'm around," I whispered as I set her in her crib and tucked the blanket up under her chin. As she drifted into sleep, I sang:

I'll be there for you.
There's no risk I wouldn't take,
No sacrifice I wouldn't make.
I'll take the world on for your sake,
And, dear, each morning when you wake
I'll be there for you.

Yours sincerely,
Walt

November 2

Dear Ed,

The ancient Greeks said, "Those whom the gods love, die young." It would appear the gods are very fond of chickens. I've never raised a bird to middle age around here. And they all die in debt. As risky enterprises go, I have found that poultry farming is right up there with Third World mining stocks and airline companies. Maggie's pretty blunt about it.

"You could find a less expensive hobby, Walt. How about Formula One racing or cocaine?"

But this year I ventured forth again. I read about the Araucana, a cross between a South American game bird and a domestic chicken. It's very hardy, and it lays blue-shelled eggs that are supposed to be cholesterol-free.

They're expensive, but I figured I could save a lot if I got hatching eggs and incubated my own laying flock. Trouble was, after the first batch, I ended up with twenty-four roosters and one hen. I ask you, what are the odds of that?

Anyway, I put them under low light in a large pen, but as soon as they got their feathers they started attacking and killing each other. Every morning I had to pull a couple of carcasses out of the pen. It was awful. It was like a leadership convention for the Conservative Party.

I found that if I let them out to free range at first light and gathered them up again after dark I could keep them from tearing each other apart. But that meant every night I had to search the apple trees with a flashlight and a feed sack for sixteen roosters.

So I decided to sell them. One morning I put one in a cage out at the road, with a sign saying "Rare South American Rooster. Five bucks." It was gone by noon. Same thing the next day. And the next. But after two weeks I shone the light up into the trees and still counted sixteen roosters. It turned out they were flying home as soon as they were let out at their new digs.

Not a bad business, really. I even had some repeat customers. But Maggie pointed out there were risks here, too. She had an ancestor who had a similar marketing strategy with horses. He trained them to come home as soon as the cheque cleared the bank. Apparently he built a flourishing trade, was known to everyone and sought after by quite a few.

"And what happened to him?" I asked.

"Well, my grandmother would only say that 'the platform collapsed under him at a public ceremony.'"

I've been thinking about those sinners in the seventh circle, and I think Dante was right. When insurance companies began, they were supposed to facilitate human achievement by cushioning it against the effects of catastrophe. But look what's happened. Our fall fair and four others around us had to be cancelled this year because the Fair Boards couldn't afford the liability insurance. The playground equipment at the school is gone. No one ever got hurt on it, but the Board of Education's insurance company found it failed to meet "modern safety standards."

And now it's becoming quite clear that we can't rebuild the Orange Hall.

I dropped in to the Red Hen Restaurant this week. When he was the clerk for Persephone Township, Harold maintained a regular table at the Red Hen. He spent hours here, receiving petitions, bestowing favours and playing euchre anytime there were four gathered together. Now that the townships have been amalgamated and everything is centralized, absolutely nothing has changed. Gertrude Lynch was sitting with him today, but I decided she might as well hear what I had to say.

"Good morning, Mr. Chairman, won't you sit down?" said Harold, in that maddeningly affable way he has.

"You can cut out the 'Mr. Chairman' stuff, Harold," I said coldly. "I resign. You knew full well there wasn't the slightest chance of getting that hall rebuilt before you appointed me. You just wanted someone else to shoulder the responsibility and take the blame when the committee came up empty-handed. We have a name for that back in the city—when you send someone off looking for something you know they're not going to find—we call it a unicorn hunt. I don't what you call it here."

"We call it a unicorn hunt. And, if I may say so, Mr. Wingfield, it's harder and harder these days to find hunters of your calibre."

I blinked and groped for a response, but none came. Seeing me speechless, Harold continued, with that bland smile fixed firmly on his face.

"I understand your frustration," he said genially. "And, of course, you're right: there was never a chance the hall could be rebuilt. But you can't just tell people that. They have to be shown the conclusion's been arrived at by due process, and the project has died a natural death."

Once again, Harold was three steps ahead of me. I felt like every time I opened my mouth with this man it was just to eat up some of the bread crumbs from the trail that he was laying down in front of me. In the meantime, Don and Freddy appeared at the door of the Red Hen. They saw me sitting with Harold and came over to check on me.

"Is this a private autopsy, or can anybody grab a scalpel?" asked Freddy.

"Be my guest," I said, and they both sat down. "This is turning into an ad hoc committee meeting anyway. The thing that baffles me is that there was no financial provision for the hall, no operations budget, no maintenance fund... it seems to me, if it hadn't burned down, it would have fallen down eventually. What was everybody thinking?"

"Oh, no, Walt," said Gertrude. "We had great plans for the hall. Last year we applied for a Heritage grant to completely restore it. It would have been just like new, but there would have been a beautiful plaque commemorating my father... and, of course, the others. But, alas, you can't restore a building that doesn't exist."

"Indeed," said Harold. "I wrote the application. It was comprehensive, if I do say so myself—more for a reconstruction than just a renovation. It was a beautiful application, and a cruel turn of fate that thwarted it."

The Orange Hall wasn't a dangerous place. The well water was fine for watering the grass and washing the floors; everyone knew you didn't drink it. The septic system was okay for emergencies, just not for heavy use; everyone knew you went to the bathroom before you went to the hall. The Clarke brothers handled handicapped access. They're two big, brawny guys who can whisk a wheelchair up the steps as smoothly as Clark Gable sweeping Vivien Leigh up the grand staircase. They look a bit like Clark Gable, too. A number of young women have been known to twist their ankles in the parking lot just to gain handicapped access to the hall.

"It's just so frustrating," I said. "You need the building to get the grant, and you need the grant to get the building."

We all sat in silence for a moment, and then Freddy finally spoke.

"What if it hadn't burned down?" he wondered.

"Well, I can speak to that," said Harold. "You wouldn't need the rezoning because it would be a renovation of a nonconforming pre-existing use."

"Yeah, but what about the water and the septic?"

"You would still have to do that, but the timeline wouldn't be as demanding. And, of course, there was provision for it in the grant application."

Don raised his hand off his chin. "What about the other stuff—parking, lighting and the handicapped access?" he asked.

"Nonconforming pre-existing use covers a broad spectrum . . . lots of wiggle room on that stuff." Harold smiled knowingly. "Besides, I made sure there were funds for that in the budget for the grant. It was a lovely application."

Gertrude wrinkled her forehead and looked at Harold. "Well, then, if it hadn't burned down, and we got the grant, what else would we need?"

"Let me see . . ." said Harold, thinking carefully. "We'd need . . . a building permit. I have one right here . . . if it hadn't burned down."

"Yes," I interrupted impatiently. "And if pigs had wings they'd be eagles. Could we get back to reality here? The fact is—it did burn down."

Freddy looked up at the ceiling fan. "Did it?" he asked.

"What do you mean, 'did it?' Of course it did."

"I dunno," said Freddy doubtfully. "There was a lot of smoke. Kinda hard to see."

I glanced at Don in exasperation. But he wasn't paying any attention to me. He was looking at Freddy.

"Yeah," he said. "Smoke damage always makes that stuff look worse than it is. Hard to say how much structural damage there might have been."

"You know, sometimes it's amazing what a cleanup and a good coat of paint will do," agreed Gertrude.

I couldn't believe this. "Cleanup? Coat of paint? There's nothing to paint. It's a pile of ashes!" I exclaimed.

Don finally looked at me. "You know that," he said. "And we know that. The question is, who else knows that?"

"Who else? Why, everybody. It was in the paper, for Pete's sake!"

"He's right," said Freddy. "What's the circulation of the paper these days?"

"Pretty high in the summer," said Harold. "But a lot less at this time of the year with the weekenders gone. Maybe...fifty-seven. And most of those are at the bottom of the birdcage by Friday. But that's a good point. We'll have to get Ed to print a retraction."

I said, "You can't be serious. The chairman of the Heritage Commission is our own member of parliament. Surely he must know—"

"Not necessarily," said Harold. "Windy Hallet's been under the weather recently."

"Oh? With what?"

"Rideau Fever," explained Freddy. "A lot of fellas come down with it when they move to Ottawa and get the government car and the expense account."

"We don't see much of Windy anymore, that's for sure," agreed Harold. "A lot of people are saying that."

"I can't believe this. Are you seriously suggesting we defraud the government by filing a false application?"

"'Defraud' is a strong word, Walt," said Harold mildly. "The application is already filed, and it was bona fide when we filed it. In the meantime, a small hiccup has occurred that creates a bit of a gap between perception and reality. I think the committee is suggesting we put perception on hold for a while and let reality catch up."

"You are!" I said rising from the table. "You're seriously suggesting we mount some kind of massive conspiracy to pretend that the Orange Hall fire never happened!"

Gertrude pursed her lips and flashed a look at me. "We could try to, Walt. Or I suppose we could let those two doddering old Orangemen bulldoze the lot and put up 'a couple of nice bungalows' while we sit around the Red Hen Restaurant picking the flyshit out of the pepper."

"That sounds like a motion," said Harold. "Would you care to put that to a vote, Mr. Chairman?"

Of course I was outvoted, and I probably should have resigned. But I didn't. Not only that, but, as I'm still chairman, I'm expected to lobby our member of parliament, Winston Hallet, the chairman of the Heritage Commission, to speed along approval of the grant. Well, that's okay. The sooner reality catches up with perception here, the easier I'll breathe.

By the way, Ed, if you're keeping score...fraud is also in the seventh circle of the Inferno. At least I'm not getting any lower. Not yet.

Yours sincerely,
Walt

November 8

Dear Ed,

Hope is still getting these ear infections, and yesterday Maggie and I drove her into the doctor's for a consultation. I thought we'd come away with another round of antibiotics, but this time the doctor showed us a diagram of an infant's inner ear.

"What we're dealing with here is a rather stubborn otitis media, an inflammation of the middle ear. Now, there are two schools of thought on this. One is that, in most cases, the infection will respond to the antibiotics and eventually clear up. On the other hand, there are stubborn cases, of which this may be one, where surgery is the best course."

"Surgery?" I said, alarmed.

"Yes," said Dr. Brigham. "We install little tubes, called myringotomy tubes, that drain the infection from the eardrum."

"But you say there's a chance with the antibiotics it could just go away."

"Most of the time it does," agreed the doctor. "There is some risk involved whichever way we decide to go."

"What kind of risk?"

"It's really a matter of the child's hearing. The tubes themselves can cause scarring and reduce the range of hearing...slightly. On the other hand, if the infection doesn't respond to the antibiotics, becomes severe and spreads, it could result in a condition called mastoiditis. It's rare, but it does occur. In that case, we would have to operate immediately, and there is a good chance the child could lose her hearing entirely."

"What do you think we should do, Doctor?"

"In this sort of case, I lean towards the surgery. But there doesn't appear to be any immediate danger. Why don't you think about it, and we'll see you next week. In the meantime, let me know if you see any change...fever, irritability, any redness or swelling."

We went out to the parking lot and walked over to the 4×4. Maggie, who had said almost nothing during the interview, now asked me why I was being quiet.

"I just don't know what to do," I said. "How do we know which is the right choice?"

"If there's any danger she might lose her hearing, we have to do the surgery, don't you think?"

"But he said the tubes might reduce her hearing."

"He said 'slightly.' What is it, Walt?" She came around to face me.

"I don't know," I sighed. "Both options have risks. For Hope, I want the other option—the one with no risks. I just don't want to pull another Flying W."

"Life is full of risks, Walt, you know that. It's the same as the business with the Orange Hall. If you try to make life risk-free, you end up not living it."

Freddy pulled up beside us in his truck.

"Say, Walt," he grinned. "I think you should come up and see what Dave is doing with your horse."

Maggie patted me on the arm. "You go ahead, Walt. I'm going to get on the Internet and see what I can find out about otitis media."

When we got to Freddy's, Dave was doing a warm-up lap with Dividend on Freddy's dirt track out behind the barn. He had her hooked up to the sulky, and she looked terrific with the breeze streaming through her mane and her head high; I've never seen her happier. There was something odd about her bridle—she didn't seem to have one. I asked Freddy how he had done it.

"He started off riding her," explained Freddy. "No bridle, no reins, nothing—just around the corral. After a while he put the bellyband on her. Then he hooked up the shafts of the sulky to the bellyband and just let her stand there. And then he started riding her with the sulky behind. And then, finally, he got off her and sat on the sulky. As long as she has nothing touching her head and no lines or reins, she's fine."

"How does he steer?"

Freddy raised his eyebrows. "He whispers to her," he said.

Dave and Dividend picked up speed as they passed in front of us. Freddy clicked the stopwatch.

"We're not out of the woods here, Walt," he warned. "We have to get her to do this at the track."

"You think she should race?"

"Look at her, Walt. It's what she's born to do. Not to mention the fact that this horse is fast. You were complaining that this community doesn't have money. This is a horse that could turn around the Larkspur gross domestic product—in a heartbeat."

"Really?" I said. "So, Dave can drive her at the track and just whisper to her, right?"

"Yeah, and we'll tell all the other drivers and the twelve hundred people in the stands to please keep quiet—Dave has to whisper to his horse. It's no good, Walt. She might as well be deaf out there."

"So, what can you do?"

Freddy glanced at Willy. "Show him," he said.

Willy uncoiled a garden hose and showed me a bottle of horse liniment.

"We're trying an ancient herbal therapy—it's called Absorbine Junior. A few dabs on her back. Makes her itchy. She wants to race anyhow; now, she's itching to race. She does her race lap and gets a shower with the hose. Itch gone. We do it a few times. The horse learns the sequence: itch, run the race, shower. And it's all positive reinforcement. She likes the itch; she loves the race; and she really loves the shower. And the best part of it is, it's actually legal."

By this time Dave was well into Dividend's race training lap. They rounded the clubhouse turn and thundered by us. Freddy clicked the stopwatch and sent Willy into action.

"Okay, Willy, hose her down quick!"

Dividend turned on a dime and trotted over to Willy, who stuck his thumb on the end of the hose and doused her, head to tail and back. Dividend shook her head and whinnied in girlish glee. Dave jumped out of the cart.

"What does the stopwatch say, Uncle Freddy?"

Freddy held it up, and his hand started to shake. "It says…it says…oh, my sufferin' sainted sister. It says that our dirt farmin' days of poverty are about to end! Now, boys, we want to be real, real careful with this horse. We don't want to try to bring her along too fast. I mean, we wouldn't want to, like, put her in the first race at Demeter Downs next Saturday."

"Nooo, we sure wouldn't want to do that," agreed Dave. "Would we, Willy?"

"Heavens, no. How about the fourth race?"

I wished them good luck and turned to go, but Freddy stopped me.

"You're coming too, Walt," he said.

"I'm not much of a racing fan, Freddy," I protested. "I'll leave it in your capable—"

"No, Walt, this is about the Orange Hall application. You can't track down Windy Hallet at the office. But he never misses a Saturday at Demeter Downs in Port Petunia. He has a box in the stands, and as far as the business of the constituency is concerned, that's where it all happens. We'll pick you up at seven Saturday morning."

Yours sincerely,
Walt

November 12

Dear Ed,

Saturday was classic late autumn. One moment the sun shone bravely, lighting up the last patches of crimson and gold on the hills. The next moment, heavy grey clouds scudded in off the lake and the hills turned dark again. The forecast was "changeable," which, of course, is weather-manese for "we dunno."

It was one of those days that could go either way. I understand Napoleon said something to that effect heading into the Battle of Waterloo. I just hoped I wasn't heading into my own Waterloo as I prepared to lie to my member of parliament, speak in support of a fraudulent grant application and encourage the Heritage Commission to incriminate itself.

When we got to Demeter Downs, we got Dividend into her box stall, and Willy and Dave went to work, rubbing her down and wrapping her forelegs, preparing her for her debut on the track.

Freddy pointed up into the stands. "There's your target, Walt—that box up there with the red and white bunting. That's the constituency office during the racing season, and I see old Windy himself just blew in."

Winston Hallet is approaching the end of his second term as the member for Hillhurst County. He's never been considered cabinet material because he's a bit of a loose cannon. They put him in charge of a few harmless things, like the House Committee on Ethics in Banking, and they made him chair of the Heritage Commission.

With some trepidation, I climbed the stairs, joined in the line of petitioners and waited my turn. I waited through the first race and the second and third races. The trumpet was just sounding for the fourth race when I finally got my chance. Hallett was a rotund man with a shiny bald pate and a fringe of snow white hair around his ears. He grabbed me enthusiastically in a warm handshake.

"How are YOU! Come on and sit down, young fella!"

It gave me the feeling that we actually knew each other from somewhere, but I couldn't think where that might be. "Hi. I'm Walt Wingfield," I introduced myself.

"Oh, I KNOW, I know, I know. You're from..."

"Larkspur," I prompted.

"Oh, I know, I know, I know. Tell me, how are things down there? How's my old friend John Drinkwater?"

"John?" I said. "Not very well, actually. He died last September."

"No! Oh, that's too bad. I hadn't heard about that. And how about my old pal Ross McNabb—still in the beef business?"

"Ross died about two years ago, in fact."

"Oh, my...and his wife, Vera...is she still...?"

"Yes, still dead," I said.

Windy picked up his field glasses and looked out over the track. "Well, here they come." The horses were coming around for the start of the fourth race.

So far so good. Evidently, Windy was a couple of laps off the pace when it came to current events in Larkspur. Of course, that didn't mean he hadn't heard about the fire.

The starting truck was bringing the horses around in formation, gathering speed as they approached the start line. It wasn't hard to pick out Dividend. Dave's Department of Highways orange vest and pink dirt bike helmet stood out sharply from the row of designer racing silks on the other drivers. They swept past the grandstand; Dividend looked terrific, head high, eyes bright; she was having the time of her life. Suddenly, the sun broke through the clouds and all things seemed positive. I took a deep breath and popped the question.

"Have you heard anything about the Orange Hall in Larkspur?"

Hallett looked at me sharply. "Of course I have," he said.

"You have?" I ventured. Bread crumbs, I thought. Just drop a bread crumb and see how he takes it.

"It is a beautiful building," he said finally.

"It is? I mean, yes, it is. We have an application in for a Heritage grant to do a restoration. Has it crossed your desk yet?"

"Oh, for sure. I was just looking at that last week. Lovely stonework in that building."

"Actually, it was a . . . I mean, it is a wood frame. Golly, it must have been . . . it went up like a . . . I mean, they built it very quickly."

"And folks feel pretty good that you're fixing it up, do they?"

"Oh, absolutely. And the committee's going like a house on . . . that is, the idea has really caught fire . . . caught on. What I mean is, everybody is very enthusiastic."

Hallett turned back to me with a puzzled frown. "Now, hang on just a minute, did you say 'fire'? I just remembered . . ."

A chill wind rustled the bunting; a dark cloud snuffed out the sun; a couple of big raindrops thudded on the roof of the box.

"I just remembered...I have a little money on a horse in this race named Firebrand; I don't want to miss it." He raised his field glasses to watch the race.

The horses were turning to the back stretch. I saw Dave's pink helmet in the middle of the pack. Dividend was moving ahead fast, and the announcer was calling her name. Now she was in front. She was winning. The rain drumming on the roof of the box drowned out the announcer's voice, and I lost sight of the horses. Then it brightened again and the horses came back into sight, rounding the turn for home. I couldn't see Dividend. One by one they flashed past the grandstand. No Dividend. She'd just disappeared in that shower...Aaah! Shower! She's had her shower; she thinks the race is over. She's probably headed home.

"By gollies, looks like there's a runaway," said Hallett, pointing to the backfield.

I snatched up his field glasses and scanned the track. I picked up a flash of orange and pink near the stables and saw Dividend trotting gaily through the backfield towards the parking lot, pursued by a posse of trainers, stewards and grooms. The parking arm was blocking the exit onto the road. Surely, I thought, that would stop her. It didn't. She crashed through, lost one wheel of the sulky on a fire hydrant and the other on the bumper of a parked car—a police cruiser. Dave bounced along on the gravel behind her, his arms waving and his mouth wide open. He was not whispering now.

Windy was waving his race ticket.

"How about that?" he crowed. "I picked a winner! Firebrand came home in a romp. And I thought I might get burned. Ha, ha, ha! Looks like you brought me good luck, Mr. . . . uh . . ."

"Wingfield."

"Oh, I KNOW, I know, I know," he assured me, grabbing my hand and pumping it again. "Thank you so much. Now, I'm going to look into that grant application just as soon as I get back to Ottawa. We'll see if we can't move it along for you." The next petitioner moved into the box. "And how are YOU, young fella? How are things in Glockamorra, mmm? Oh, I KNOW, I know, I know . . ."

And with that, my audience with the great man was over.

Thankfully, Dave and Dividend are both going to be all right. Even the sulky wasn't a total writeoff. They were able to use the shafts as a temporary splint for Dave's leg.

Yours sincerely,
Walt

November 16

Dear Ed,

Three days later we were back at the doctor's. He said Hope's okay for now, but we shouldn't wait too long to decide what to do. It seems the symptoms of otitis media vary a lot, and sometimes it's hard to diagnose how serious it is.

On our way back through Larkspur, I noticed a group of people standing in front of the Red Hen Restaurant—Harold, Gertrude, Freddy and Don—so I pulled over to the curb. It looked like another impromptu meeting of the ad hoc committee.

Harold looked up as I opened the car door. "Morning, Walt," he said cheerily. "We've got some good news...and some other news."

"Oh?" I said. "What's the good news?"

"I got a call from the Heritage Commission this morning. They say the grant's been approved for the full amount. They're sending us a cheque. It's going to arrive today."

"Today? That's terrific! The full amount? Today? I can't believe it. Listen, everybody. I'm sorry I was so negative about that 'perception–reality' thing. I'm just hopelessly old-fashioned, I guess. I had some paranoid notion we'd find ourselves at the centre of an Auditor General's investigation. What's the other news?"

"Windy Hallett is delivering the cheque personally," said Harold. "He's coming down by train. He wants to kick off his re-election campaign by having his picture taken in front of the Orange Hall."

"I knew it!" I shouted. "We'll be caught. We're all going to jail! I told you this was crazy!"

If Harold was concerned, he showed no sign of it. "We've been discussing it, Walt. He's just coming to have his picture taken."

"In front of the Orange Hall, which, may I remind you, does not exist."

"Certainly that does present a challenge."

That seemed to me to be the understatement of the decade.

"It gets dark about 5:45," said Maggie. "It would help if it was dark."

"Yeah," said Don. "And it would help if he didn't have his glasses."

"And it would help if he was drunk," added Freddy.

"I suppose," I said. "But we can't count on any of those things. Who's going to meet him at the station?"

"He appears to assume it will be you, Mr. Chairman," said Harold. "We were thinking maybe you could pick him up in your 4×4. He'll be on the 4:15."

"Really? I was actually thinking of leaving town on that train. Anyway, why would I pick him up in the car? We can walk to the hall from the station; it's just across the bridge."

Maggie took me by the elbow back to the car and handed Hope to me. "Bring him over in the 4×4, Walt. It will be all right. In the meantime, you take Hope down to the farm and get her settled. I'll come down and spell you off when you have to leave."

This often happens to me up here. I listen to the same conversation as everyone else and I watch them all lift off in the same direction in a common cause, leaving me—the last starling on the fence—without the faintest idea what just happened.

When I drove into the station parking lot, there was a light drizzle falling and the weather had turned cold. The train pulled in right on time. Windy stepped down onto the platform.

"And how are YOU, young fella? How are your two front feet?" he asked heartily, pumping my hand.

"Hi, Mr. Hallett. I'm Walt Wingfield."

"Oh, I know, I know, I know...you're my lucky fireman, ho, ho, ho." This time he did actually seem to remember me. I got him settled in the 4×4. As we pulled out of the parking lot, I took a deep breath.

"Listen, Mr. Hallett, there's something I should probably explain to you before we..."

And then I saw the fire truck sitting at the bridge with its lights flashing and men in yellow rainsuits standing about. One of them walked over to us and tapped on the window. It was Don.

"G'day, sir," he said, leaning in the window. "We got us a little problem with the bridge here, and we're gonna have to send you the long way round to get to the hall. Just follow the signs and keep to the left."

I turned left and we followed Mill Street, which goes steeply downhill to make the loop around Dry Cry's store, the fuel depot and a row of old factory buildings that are finally being renovated to house various local arts and crafts. Another knot of people in rain slickers stood in the middle of the road and waved us to a halt. A face appeared at the window. It was Freddy.

"Hi there, your honour. We were thinking that, while you're in the fair town of Larkspur, you might just take a minute to have a tour of our newest industry—the Pine Springs Micro-Brewery. Just opened last month."

"Oh, by gollies, I read about that in the papers," said Windy. "I think we have a minute, don't we, Mr. Wingfield?"

I shrugged and said, "Sure, by all means."

We got out of the car and Freddy led us over to the door. Freddy steered Windy inside and began the cook's tour of the brewery.

"You know, they have sixteen different varieties they make right here on the premises. But you can't get them in Ottawa yet. Made with the finest local ingredients. One hundred years of brewing experience...about one month with an actual licence."

"Sixteen varieties, you say?" marvelled Windy.

"Yeah," said Freddy, handing him a tall glass. "Here's the first one. It's called Strongarm."

We were there for over an hour while Windy sampled all sixteen. We poured him back into the car at 5:30, just as the light started to fade. We followed the River Road for another few hundred yards, and then I heard the unmistakable sound of the steam calliope coming from the fairgrounds up ahead. Sure enough, as we rounded the bend, we saw people at the gate. I smelled popcorn and hot dogs and saw a row of black-and-white dairy calves being led in the gate by young kids. The Larkspur Fair seemed to be in full swing. Suddenly, Gertrude Lynch appeared beside the car.

"Why, Mr. Hallett," she cried. "What a wonderful surprise! You're just in time for the opening ceremonies. Everyone will be just thrilled to see you on the platform."

Windy made straight for the grandstand, where Isobel Meadows was receiving her crown as the Fair Queen. He huffed up the stairs, put his arm around Isobel and gave her a big kiss. The crowd cheered. A voice called out for a speech, and Windy was happy to oblige.

"I want to thank yas all for coming out," he hiccupped into the microphone. "You know, it's a great thing when you have a group of hard-working volunteers to put on a good little fair like they do here in...in..."

"Larkspur," prompted Gertrude.

"...Larkspur! I remember the day when I brought my pig to this fair when I was just the same age as these young people down here in front of the stage. I polished up that pig with buttermilk until he was so bright you pretty near needed a pair of sunglasses just to look at him. And I was so proud when I got a white ribbon for third place, it was like they crowned me king, so it was..."

Windy rang all the changes...agriculture is the backbone of the country, the government can and will do more to help the small producer, and if you ate breakfast this morning you should thank a farmer. Then he lambasted the firearms registry, which, by the way, he voted for in his first term.

"You know the difference between a boat anchor and the Gun Registry, do you? Well, you would normally tie a rope on the boat anchor before you throw it overboard, ho, ho, ho!

"I think you all know I'm not a man to forget his friends in the constituency. My opponents have called it dipping into the pork barrel. Well, I call it bringing home the bacon!

"You know," he said, passing a hand over his face and looking serious for a moment. "It was a terrible thing when they gave women the vote. But, God help them, they've done it, and we're just going to have to...what's that you say?"

Gertrude was tugging on his arm now and guiding him off the stage. "They want your picture with the Fair Queen and the grand champion calf," she said. "Come and help, Isobel. This way, your honour."

Isobel took his arm and smiled sweetly at him as she guided him down the platform steps. "Oh, Mr. Hallett, you'd look so much handsomer without your glasses.

Here, let me hold them for you." Windy missed the last step on the grandstand and stumbled into the side of young Donny's prize calf, who took no notice and went on chewing its cud. Windy bounced back into the arms of two spectators.

"My, that's a wild calf you got there, young man," he sputtered. "Can you not get her quieted down?"

He grabbed the calf's ear for support. It shook its head and moved forward six inches, and there was an audible crunch of broken glass. Isobel looked crestfallen as she handed him the broken frames.

"I'm so sorry, Mr. Hallett. Donny's calf stepped on your glasses."

"Not to worry, my dear, I have another pair at home. But they're not as nice as the pair on you. I mean, your glasses, ho, ho, ho!"

We took the picture and supported Windy back to the 4×4. By now it was dark.

"Gertrude," I whispered. "If the bridge is closed, how do I get him across the river?"

"They've rigged up the old cable ferry for you, your honour," said Gertrude. "Keep bearing to the left and you'll see the old crossing."

"Left again?" mumbled Windy. "If we go any further left, we'll end up sitting with the NDP."

Down at the river crossing, a hooded figure stood on the deck of the cable ferry, his hand on the winch, waving the 4×4 onto the barge—an aged man whose hair was white...who was, in fact, the Squire. He raised an arm in salute.

"I come to lead you to the other shore," he called.

We crossed the river in a blanket of fog, in silence broken only by the creaking of the old winch and Windy singing softly to himself.

Yes, we will gather at the river,
the beautiful, the beautiful, the river...

We bumped against the shore, and I drove off the ferry onto a rough track that wound up the side of the hill. At the crest, we emerged from the fog and drove out under the stars. There was a light. And there in front of us was the Orange Hall. In three hours, the community had rebuilt the hall.

When I looked closer, I saw that it was just scaffolding shrouded with plastic; they'd put up scaffolding in the shape of the hall. I hurried Windy around to the front, where the light was coming from a row of floodlights, illuminating the facade. Here, there was a gap in the scaffolding and an actual structure—part of a wall, a set of steps and a doorway with the old sign fixed above it: LOL Number 26, Larkspur 1954. It wasn't the Orange Hall, but it did look familiar. A small group of people waited to welcome Windy. At the front was Harold.

"So good of you to come, Mr. Hallett," he said in his most courtly manner. "Everyone is so pleased and excited to see you. Now, just stand up here and we can take your picture."

I was right next to the facade now. I looked down and saw some printing stamped at the corner of the plywood—Larkspur Little Theatre. That's why I recognized it! It was the set from last summer's production of *The Perils of Persephone*. It was just a plywood set piece.

"We must go inside and have a look," insisted Windy.

Harold moved in front of him. "No, no, no, Mr. Hallett, we can't do that."

"Oh," said Windy. "And why not?"

For the first time, Harold wavered. "Because... because..." He turned to me. "Mr. Chairman, tell him why not."

The inspiration came like a bolt out of the blue. "Because of insurance," I said triumphantly. "Yes, insurance! Why, we'd need hard hats, steel-toed boots, safety glasses, breathing masks... The safety railings aren't installed and, of course, waivers would have to be signed..."

Windy instantly relented. "Ah, yes, insurance," he said. "Say no more. I understand. We'll just have to make do with a picture. I have the cheque here. Who should I give this to?"

"To everybody," I shouted. "C'mon, everyone, crowd in here. Harold, Don, Gertrude, Freddy..." They all crowded in around me, and the flashbulbs popped.

— • —

When I got back home, the house was dark; Maggie and Hope weren't there. I found a scribbled note from Maggie on the kitchen table. It read: "Elma is driving us to Emergency at Hillhurst Regional Hospital. Mastoiditis."

I called Spike and herded him quickly to the 4×4. Hope would need him. At the hospital, we found them in the recovery room. I spoke to the doctor briefly. He said the surgery had been successful, but we'd have to wait until

Hope came out of the anesthetic to know whether she was all right.

Maggie was worn out, asleep in the chair beside the bed. Spike settled beside her on the floor and put his head on her foot. I sat with Hope and sang softly to her, the lullaby she might not ever hear again.

I'll be there for you.
There's no risk I wouldn't take...

But I couldn't finish it, because it wasn't true. The fact is, I wasn't there for her. I didn't take the risk. I just abandoned Hope...

Spike looked at me reproachfully. "Woof," he said. Hope's eyes blinked open. "'pike!" she cried.

I breathed a sigh of relief and sent a prayer heavenward.

Yours sincerely,
Walt

Another note from the editor:
So that's how it went.

Over the next few weeks, the new hall was framed, roofed and bricked, and the gap between perception and reality was closed. Walt stepped off the Hall Committee about the same time Ernie and Gertrude came to blows over the cost of the new cupboards.

Shortly after the election was called, I got Windy's campaign brochure in the mail. "Winston Hallett's Vision for the Future: It Doesn't Get Any Better." Politicians aren't normally given to such brutal candour.

Freddy, Willy and Dave aren't giving up on Dividend. They're trying to breed her for the next addition to the line of the great Clipper Ship. They just need to find a stallion fast enough to catch up with her.

I have a picture on my desk. It shows a big crowd of maybe fifty people standing in front of the new hall, watching a crane hoisting a heavy cast-iron bell into a square tower on the south peak of the roof. They found it when they were cleaning up the debris in the basement. Gertrude said it was donated when the old hall was built, but at the time, they didn't have the money to put up a bell tower.

Now that it's finally on the building, they ring it for every important event, like a fiftieth wedding anniversary or someone bowling a perfect game or a winning lottery ticket.

People call it the Cowbell. In the absence of any fine sculpture or great architecture, it helps remind us who we are. Of course, the insurance company has told us they don't insure bell towers and if it falls off the building and kills somebody, we're not covered.

It's unfortunate, but we're just going to have to live with that risk.